A Kingpin's Ambition 2

Lock Down Publications &
Ca$h Presents
A Kingpin's Ambition 2

Lock Down Publications
P.O. Box 1482
Pine Lake, Ga 30072-1482

Visit our website at **www.lockdownpublications.com**

First Edition July 2017
Printed in the United States of America
This is a work of fiction. Names, characters, places, and incidents either are products of the author's imagination or are used fictitiously. Any similarity to actual events or locales or persons, living or dead, is entirely coincidental.

Cover design and layout by: Dynasty's Cover Me
Book interior design by: Shawn Walker
Edited by: Mia Rucker

Stay Connected with Us!

Text **LOCKDOWN** to 22828 to stay up-to-date with new releases, sneak peaks, contests and more...

Thank you!

Submission Guideline.

Submit the first three chapters of your completed manuscript to ldpsubmissions@gmail.com, subject line: Your book's title. The manuscript must be in a .doc file and sent as an attachment. Document should be in Times New Roman, double spaced and in size 12 font. Also, provide your synopsis and full contact information. If sending multiple submissions, they must each be in a separate email.

Have a story but no way to send it electronically? You can still submit to LDP/Ca$h Presents. Send in the first three chapters, written or typed, of your completed manuscript to:

LDP: Submissions Dept
Po Box 1482
Pine Lake, Ga 30072

DO NOT send original manuscript. Must be a duplicate.

Provide your synopsis and a cover letter containing your full contact information.

Thanks for considering LDP and Ca$h Presents.

Ambitious

Chapter One

"Hey, how y'all doin'? My name Sabrina. If y'all need some help wit' anything or whenever y'all get ready to checkout, just let me know and I'll take care of y'all," the cute little salesgirl said with a smile when Killa and Tiara walked into the urban clothing store in Greenbriar Mall.

"Check that," Killa drawled smoothly as they casually made their way to the wall of women's tennis shoes. Tiara absentmindedly sung the words to Ray J's old hit *One Wish* as it began to play from the speakers throughout the store. "Bring yo' fat ass on over here and sit down," he teased.

Tiara sucked her teeth. "Shut up, nigga, yo' ass the one that made me like this." She giggled happily as she waddled over to the bench and sat down, sighing heavily. "I'll be so damn glad when this lil girl decide she ready to come on out," she said while rubbing her seven month and two week pregnant belly.

"You and me both. A nigga gettin' kinda tired of them same ol' positions," Killa joked and jumped back to avoid the slap Tiara tried to give him while he chuckled. "I'm just playin', bae, damn. You know I can't get enough of that blackberry," he lowered his voice and said.

Tiara glared at him for a second before rolling her eyes. "Yeah whatever, nigga, yo' ass go eat it like you can't, too, soon as we get home," she said in mock anger.

He laughed. "You say that shit like that's some kind of punishment or somethin'. You know damn well I dont mind. Matter-of-fact, I'll eat it now if you bad enough to let me," he said while reaching for her crotch but she swatted his hand away with a giggle.

"Move, boy. Oooh, I like them," she said and pointed to a pair of pink and white Bo Jackson's on the wall.

A little while later, Killa signaled for the salesgirl to come over and she approached with a bright, pretty smile. "Hey, y'all need some help wit' somethin'?" she chirped.

"Uhh, yeah, we wanna see these eight in a size eleven."

"Nigga, you know I don't wear no damn eleven," Tiara exploded, looking at Killa like he had lost his mind.

Laughing again, he said, "I'm just fuckin' wit' ya, bae. Let us see 'em in a six."

The salesgirl stared at all of the shoes for a second before she spoke. "Y'all wanna see all of these?" she asked hesitantly with a slight smile at the playfulness of the man.

"Yeah, somethin' wrong wit' that?" Tiara responded with a smidget of an attitude.

"Nah. I'll be back in a minute," she said, her smile growing as she hurried away, thinking about the big ass commission she was possibly about to make.

It took two trips to bring all eight pairs of the shoes from the storeroom. She just so happened to be stopping by to check on her two customers when she saw the handsome guy with long dreads dig in his pocket and pull out something that twinkled repeatedly as the lights in the store danced off of it.

Already on one knee because he'd been helping Tiara slip in and out of her shoes, Killa had decided that it was as good a time as any to take the plunge. "Tiara Marche Jackson, I love the hell out yo' black ass, girl." Sabrina, the salesgirl, inhaled sharply and stared in wide eyed awe at the romantic scene unfolding in front of her. Tiara used both of her hands to cover her gaping mouth. "We done been through hell and back and through all that shit, yo' black ass always been right there when I needed ya. That's how I know I want me and you to spend the rest of our life together, shawdy."

"Uh-uhnn, wait a minute, nigga, what you doin'? Please tell me what the fuck you doin' baby," Tiara exclaimed quietly, tears running from her eyes as she bounced and fidgeted uncontrollably with excitement.

"I want you to be my wife, girl. Will you marry me, baby?"

Stunned speechless with joy, she stared into Killa's eyes for a long moment, her tears falling rapidly, before she nodded. "Yes, baby." It came out in a hoarse whisper. "Yes," she exclaimed and wrapped her arms around his neck.

Sabrina and a couple of the other salesgirls and customers in the store clapped in girlish excitement when he slipped the one and a half carat solitaire diamond engagement ring on her finger. "I love you, Teet," he said and kissed her lips.

"I love you, too, baby," Tiara said, holding up her hand to get a good look at the monstrous diamond on her finger.

"Oh yeah, we wanna get all of these, too," Killa said to Sabrina, motioning towards all of the shoes as he helped Tiara to her feet before they headed to the register.

***

"Y'all can put him in seven hunnid, I'ma come get him in a minute," the Fulton County Jail correctional officer said over the intercom to two of his coworkers. They'd just brought Chop back up to the seventh floor from the holding cells downstairs where he'd been waiting ever since being brought back from interrogation at Atlanta Police Headquarters. "What's up, Johnson? You must have got some bad news, bruh," Davidson, the young C.O. from Etheridge said as he stepped into 700 with a handcuff key in hand, motioning for Chop to turn around so he could uncuff him.

Chop sighed and shook his head. "Somethin' like that. What's for lunch?" he asked gloomily, rubbing his wrists.

"Some bullshit you ain't go eat it. Ya pahtna wit' the dreads sent ya another pack, though. I got it up there in the tower. I'ma get it to ya before I dip."

Chop nodded. "'Preciate it. Where you seen that nigga at?"

"I had bumped into him and that ho Tiara from Fif Ward at the BP on West Lake. I ain't know she was bruh baby mama, man. She some action, bruh. He ain't got his self nothin'."

Chop chuckled and shook his head. "You must be done fucked that ho, too?"

"Hell naw, but a couple of my pahtnas say they used to be smashin' her and that lil ho Hot and some mo' of them Fif' Ward ho's. Bruh fucked up when he put a baby in that ol' sack chasin' ass bitch."

"You know they been had another baby before now, right? They got a lil boy together, too."

"Damn, I ain't know that shit. Bruh done went out bad twice."

Chop laughed. "Man, I'm gone. Fuck wit' me before ya leave, man," he said as he walked to Dorm 500.

"I got ya, man," Davidson said.

When Chop walked into his housing unit, he saw his young pahtna Crack Baby from Leila Valley standing up under the TV talking shit. As soon as he spotted Chop, he cut what he was saying short and rushed over to him. "What's hap'nin, big homie? What them ho's talkin' 'bout?" he asked excitedly with hopes that his pahtna had gotten some good news.

"Same ol' shit, man, trying to get a nigga to fold. Talkin' 'bout twenty and shit."

Crack Baby winced. "You gotta stand up, big bruh, twenny on drugs ain't but like four or five years, then you can make parole, but you might catch a sweet plea, though. I talked to my cousin earlia, shawdy say ya pahtna out there eatin', bruh, and homes fuckin' wit' ya the long way," Crack Baby nodded. "You might have to just take ya lick, bruh, you know Killa and the rest of them Boulevard niggas go take care of ya while you down the road. You can't eat no cheese, though, fool. Rats get exterminated."

Chop frowned slightly as he started to make his way to his cell. "C'mo, bruh, I ain't tellin' them people shit. They ass just go have to do they damn job 'cause I ain't 'bout do it for them. They can just gimme my lil time and go on and get this shit over wit', though."

Crack Baby nodded again. "That's right, fuck them bitches. If they ass wanna know somethin', make them ho's do they fuckin' job."

Chop rubbed his eyes. "I'm ti'ed as fuck, lil bruh. I'm 'bout to go lay down for a minute. I'ma smoke a stick of gas wit' ya when I get up."

"A'ight, big dog," Crack Baby said.

Chop went to his cell and closed the door behind him. "Fuck, Chop," he hissed and mashed his palms into his closed eyes. Tears were brimming in them when he opened them back and he punched the wall out of anger and frustration. He knew he'd just sold his soul and that it was no turning back, but what he didn't know was what in the fuck had possessed him to do it in the first place. Then he thought about rotting away in some prison for the next twenty or so years of his life and that quickly put a new perspective on things. Never mind the fact that he would eventually wind up sending his pahtnas to prison, at least it wouldn't be him, it couldn't be him. But still, his tears fell as he laid on his bunk thinking about Killa and the rest of his pahtnas he was about to betray while Crack Baby's words echoed repeatedly in his mind, *You can't eat no cheese, though, fool. Rats get exterminated.*

***

"What up mufucka. I need a deuce," Trayon said as he walked up to Bam, who was standing in front of the old trap spot on Linden Avenue.

Since Chop had been in jail, he had somewhat taken it over because Killa didn't want it. Sherrelle had even started getting money out of the spot, which was cool because she was fam and she brought a lot of her clientele that she didn't mind sharing.

"Bam checked the time on his phone before he responded to Trayon. "Where my money at, shawdy? I swear, man, you been walkin' 'round this bitch like you don't even owe a nigga, bruh. What's up?" he asked calmly.

"Just chill, my nigga, I got ya. I'ma straighten my face, man," Trayon said and smiled slyly as he tried to give Bam some dap.

"Well let me know when, my nigga, 'cause it damn sure don't look like you tryin' too hard to. You done came and bought some work two or three mo' times since then, bruh," he said while only looking at Trayon's extended hand.

Embarrassed by the disrespectful gesture, Trayon raised his voice a little. "Damn, my nigga, as much as you eatin' 'round this mufucka, you sweatin' a nigga 'bout a ol' chump ass thirteen hunnid, my nigga?" he asked incredulously. "I remember when we used to chase cars together, nigga, getting twenny off a hunnid. Now you handlin' a nigga all fucked up an shit. Y'all niggas been on some uppity shit lately, my nigga, facts."

Bam took a deep breath to try to calm his rising temper. Trayon had been his pahtna at one point in time, so he didn't want to overreact and cause some serious bad blood between them because at the moment, he wasn't mentally prepared to kill or even shoot him. "Bruh," he said with a confused look on his face. "How the fuck you go beat me gettin' mad 'bout my shit? I ain't ask you to come get that work from me, my nigga, you did that shit on ya own. And now 'cause we fuck wit' each other and I'm gettin' a lil money, you think you ain't gotta gimme my shit back? Negative." He shook his head and said, "Whatever money I'm gettin', my nigga, ain't got a bitch ass thing to do wit' the business me and you got goin' on, jones. But you know what, though?" He paused again and looked back at the apartment. "Gone in there and tell Loose to give ya a deuce, but I'm tellin' ya, bruh, don't come back 'round here tryin' to spend no money if you ain't got my bread."

Trayon looked at the nigga who had once been his pahtna and shook his head. "'Bout thirteen hunnid dolla's, bruh?"

"It be like that," Bam said then abruptly turned and walked away towards Parkway. A burgundy Grand Prix whipped up on him immediately and he leaned into the window as Trayon looked on with a look of obvious envy and dislike before heading into the apartment to go see Loose about the deuce of powder he needed.

"Lame ass niggas," he mumbled and shook his head.

Ambitious

Chapter Two

Killa sat on the edge of the bed smiling broadly, looking on pleasantly surprised as Tiara entertained him with a little strip tease. Thoroughly enjoying the show and extremely appreciative of just the thought of it, he looked at her sexy body through lust filled eyes, hard as a brick inside his shorts. True, Tiara was pregnant, as hell, but her body had taken on the extra pounds gracefully. Her breasts were a bit swollen but not ridiculously so, and her hips and thighs had spread beautifully. Her stomach was huge but that was to be expected seeing as to how a little person was calling that little space home for now. Her beautiful black skin, which she went to extreme lengths to keep stretch mark free, glistened softly as she tried her damndest to come off as sexy to her new fiancé. He chuckled quietly and Tiara stopped dancing immediately.

"What you laughin' at, Brenton?" She squinted her eyes and asked suspiciously, embarrassment beginning to creep through her as she looked around for the silk robe she'd shed only a few minutes earlier.

Killa knew better than to tell her how clumsy she looked trying to dance like that with her big ass belly, regardless of how much he liked it. He was smart enough to know that it would only hurt her extremely sensitive feelings, and that just wouldn't be a smart move. "Nothin', why you stop, bae?"

"'Cause you fuckin' laughin' at me 'cause I look fuckin' stupid," she pouted like a little girl.

"No you don't, bae. I liked it. You got me horny as fuck."

"You just sayin' that shit to try to make me feel..." she started saying with a disbelieving look on her face before he cut her off.

"I ain't lyin', T, I'm serious. C'mere," he said. Tiara sucked her teeth and walked slowly over to the bed. He put a hand on either side of her swollen belly and began to place soft little kisses all over it. "I think you sexier now than before you got pregnant, babe."

"Yeah, yeah, whatever, nigga. Lemme find out yo' ass got pregnant lady fettish," she joked. "But for real, though, I know you ti'ed of my fat ass." She rolled her eyes and said as a craving for some Moose Tracks ice cream with a dill pickle assaulted her.

"You ain't fat, bae, you pregnant. And if I was ti'ed of ya, I wouldn't be home at a decent time and in bed wit' yo' ass every night. You know it ain't 'bout appearance wit' me and you, bae. I love yo' black ass, T, fat or skinny, big or small. Don't never doubt that shit."

Joy radiated from Tiara's face as she tried unsuccessfully to fight back the urge to smile. "How much?" she asked.

Killa slid to his knees and slowly ran his tongue from her belly button to the blackberry tattoo just above her pussy. By the time he reached her sweet spot, she was dripping wet and beside herself with excitement. He had her bend over the edge of the bed so he could eat her pussy from the back. When he spread her ass cheeks and tongued her asshole, she came violently, letting out a high note that even Mariah would envy.

Wiping his mouth, he stood up. "I ain't done wit' yo' ass," he said gruffly, fighting to keep his desire in check. He wanted to smash her black ass, but contrary to what she, the doctors, and everybody else that she had desperately gotten to try to convince him said, he feared that if he hit the pussy the way he longed to hit it, something might go wrong with the baby. Call him what you want, but he didn't want to take any chances.

He slid into her from behind, and the way she looked back over her shoulder at him, biting her bottom lip, damn near pushed him over the edge. In no time, his dick was white with both of their fluids as he kept an upbeat tempo with his thrusts into her. Grabbing her waist, he began to grind a little with every plunge into her. Knowing him as well as she did, she knew he was close to coming, so she wiggled free from the vise grip he had on her waist and spun around. She grabbed the base of his dick and slipped the rest of him into her mouth. Gagging a couple of times from the length of him, she fell into a rhythm, working on his dick with her mouth and both of her hands to get him off.

He exploded in her mouth, but unfazed by it, she didn't stop, moaning and slurping loudly with saliva and come all over her face and hands. "I want you to hit this pussy again, daddy," Tiara said hoarsely as she jacked his semi-hard dick. She laid back and scooted to the edge of the bed before putting her legs in the air as high as her pregnant belly would allow them to go and spreading them.

Killa stood at full attention when she stuck two fingers inside of her and began to work them as she eyed him with a slutty little expression on her face. He shook his head as he thought about how beautiful she was, big stomach and all.

"What's wrong, baby?" she whispered, worried about his head shaking and hesitation.

"Nothin', bae, just thinkin' 'bout how much I love ya. That's all."

Tiara beamed. "Awww, I love you, too, baby. But now ain't exactly the time to be gettin' all lovey-dovey, boo?" she said and nodded towards her exposed sex. "Ya feel me?"

Nodding himself, Killa stepped up and slid in.

"Now smash this pussy, daddy," she commanded.

***

Beep. Beep. Beep. Beep. The machine attatched to Leena beeped loudly in the looming silence of her room at the Warm Springs Medical Center in Gwinnett County. Although she lay in her bed, quiet and unmoving, appearing to be at ease physically, mentally she was in an uproar. Unintentionally, her mind was repeatedly replaying marquee events from her life, especially events from the last few weeks before she was shot nearly nine months ago. None of it made any sense at first because none of it was clear. but slowly, her mind was able to piece together bits and pieces of her tattered memories and...

Beeeeeeeep. The machine monitoring her heart rate cried out loud enough to grab the attention of one of the night nurses and send her into a panic, searching for help. A tear leaked from the corner of one of Leena's closed eyes as she recalled that she'd been pregnant that fateful night that she'd been beaten and shot. Her eyelids fluttered and opened as she unconsciously arched her back while gasping for air.

Three nurses, accompanied by a female doctor, burst through the door of the room and rushed to her bedside. Confusion was evident on all of their faces as two nurses, one male and one female, began to check monitors and other instruments.

Looking over a clipboard she'd picked up, the doctor raised her gaze to a wild eyed, scared looking young woman, and with a warm smile she said, "Hello, Ms. Wright, welcome back."

***

"I gotta do what I gotta do," Chop whispered repeatedly to himself in an attempt to boost his nerve to slide the witness statement form requesting protective custody under the door to the officer that was making his rounds. Sighing, he dropped his head and closed his eyes. A few seconds later, his closed eyelids glowed a reddish-orange and a light metallic tapping at his door made him look up.

"What's up, bruh, you a'ight?" The C.O. asked, his head appearing in the slim window of the door.

Chop squinted to shield his eyes from the bright beam of the flashlight the officer was shining on him.

"Yeah, I'm straight, man," he answered glumly and looked down at the statement his hands were clutching.

"A'ight, I was just checkin' on ya, man. You was lookin' like you was goin' through it just then," he said and started to walk away. but a few knocks on the glass brought him right back to Chop's door.

"Man, I lied, man. I ain't a'ight." Chop held the witness statement form to the glass and then bent down to push it under the door. "You can take care of that for me, man?" he asked as the C.O. read the form.

When he finished reading the statement, he looked into Chop's eyes for a second before he spoke. "This some bullshit, shawdy. I know you. The Mobb ain't go fuck wit' you."

"Real shit, my life in danger if I stay in population, man."

The serious expression and tone of voice Chop used made the C.O. sigh and shake his head. "Why the fuck you wait 'til damn near shift change to pull this shit? You could've been did this shit, man. Pack ya shit up," he said and walked away mumbling as he finished making his rounds.

Chop leaned back against the wall and slid down to the floor while holding his head in his hands as he dropped a few tears.

***

The sound of a whining baby woke Killa from a deep, sex induced slumber. His eyes popped open and he stared disoriented at the ceiling for a second before Tiara nudged him.

"Answer that annoying ass phone," she muttered groggily. Sitting up and swinging his feet over the side of the bed, he farted when he reached to grab his phone from the nightstand. "Damn, you stank," she said to him and made a point of covering her nose with the covers.

"It can't be no worse than yours, lil mama," he said dryly.

Tiara chuckled a little. "Whatever, nigga, I'm pregnant. And who the fuck callin' yo' ass this damn early anyway?"

He shrugged. "Prob'ly one of my side bitches that want some wake up dick," he joked before feeling a slap across the back of his head immediately after the last word left his mouth.

"Don't fuckin' play wit' me, nigga," she warned.

Laughing, he glanced at the display of his Galaxy and quickly sobered up. "Shhh," he said to Tiara and stood up. "Hello?" he answered.

"Good morning, sir, Mr. Brenton James please?" a male voice said.

"This him," Killa responded, goosebumps covering every inch of his body.

"Hello, Mr. James, my name is Dr. Dean Thomas. I'm the night director at the Warm Springs Medical Center. I'm terribly sorry to bother you at such an hour but this cannot wait." Killa was silent and even if the cat didn't have his tongue, he probably still wouldn't have been able to get out a single word past the lump in his throat, but luckily the doctor kept talking. "Your fiancée, Ms. Mileena Wright, has awakened. She is awake and fully functional and has been for the past forty-five minutes to an hour or so."

Stunned beyond stupidity, Killa said the first thing that came to his mind. "What you mean awake?" he mumbled while making his way to the bathroom and closing the door behind him.

"I mean that she has recovered from her comatose state and that she is fully conscious and functioning."

Smiling, he closed his eyes and thanked God for this latest blessing. He turned the water on in the sink to cover up his sniffling sounds before opening his eyes again. Looking at his reflection in the mirror, he watched a few fat tears roll lazily down his cheeks and disappear into the dimple creases of his face. "I... I mean, like... is somethin'... what's wrong wit' her?"

"Physically, nothing. She's fine. Although she is a bit sore and weak from being bed-ridden for so long, but she has controlled movement of all limbs and extremities. Right now our resident neurologist is running some tests to let us know exactly what kind of shape her mind is in, but for the most part, she appears to be pretty sharp mentally to me."

Killa closed his eyes again because he couldn't believe his ears. For months he'd been growing more and more accustomed to Leena's absence to the point where he was now comfortable. But never once, in all of the countless days, weeks, months, did he ever even vaguely forget even the smallest thing about the woman he loved. From her cute stubby little fingers and toes to the way her beautiful green eyes sparkled when she laughed and flashed fire when she was angry, to how she smelled when she was fresh out of the bath. He recalled it all. The love of his life was back. His partner, his soul mate, he had to see her. "Can I come see her now?" he asked anxiously.

"I don't see why not. I imagine she'd be delighted to see a familiar face right now, especially yours."

Killa smiled even harder. "I'ma be there in a hour," he said, and without even waiting for a response, he disconnected the call. Drying his face, he took a deep breath to try to calm his racing heartbeat as he leaned against the sink. The knock at the door made his heart skip a beat and he snapped his gaze to the door just as Tiara waddled her pregnant, naked ass into the bathroom.

"I gotta use the..." She was saying but froze the second she saw his face. "Baby, what's wrong?" she asked with a worried tone and facial expression.

He shook his head and smiled. "Nothin', bae, everything cool."

"It don't damn look like it. It look like yo' ass been in here cryin'. What's wrong Brenton?" she asked again and in a bit firmer tone.

Still smiling, he answered. "Nothin'. Look, I'm 'bout to dip for a minute."

Tiara frowned. "Nigga, yo' ass get a phone call at six o'clock in the damn mornin' that yo' ass gotta leave out from 'round me to take, that got yo' ass in here cryin' and shit, and now you talkin' 'bout you 'bout to leave? Uh-uhn," she said with her eyes closed while shaking her head. "Hell no, muthafucka. Where the fuck you think you 'bout to go?"

"To handle some business. Don't start trippin', man. You already know I be havin' a lot goin' on."

He was right, she knew exactly what *business* meant, but this time, something, maybe the fabled *woman's intuition*, was screaming for her to not only not accept what he was saying but to fight against it with everything that she had. "I'm yo' business, too, nigga, me and this lil girl I'm carryin'," she said, while grabbing her stomach. "And I don't want you to go."

Killa frowned, but after quickly analyzing the situation, he flashed a handsome, lazy smile. He knew what was going on. Grabbing her wrist, he gently drew her to him while turning her around so her back would be against his chest. He nuzzled her neck while rubbing her stomach. "Listen, Tiara, I love you, Doon, and this baby unconditionally." A smug little smile came to her lips then, she just knew that she'd won. But then, his hold on her became firm and his voice turned as hard as a piece of steel. "But if you think for one second that I'ma tolerate you showin' ya ass and tryin' to fuckin' bully me to get yo' way just 'cause you pregnant and you got that ring on ya finger now, I'm here to tell ya," he shook his head slowly, "You got life fucked up two times, shawdy." The smile she'd been wearing just a few seconds before had now evaporated and left a sour, pinched look on her pretty, black face.

His tone softened a little when he continued. "Now, hell yeah, you my heartbeat, bae, and I'ma do whatever to make, and keep ya happy. But when I tell ya I got business, it ain't for you to be questionin' me, or it, 'cause I'm doin' what I'm s'posed to be doin' for our lil family. Now tell me, man, can you rock wit' that?"

Reluctantly, Tiara nodded, but in her mind, she knew he wasn't talking about shit. She knew that she would continue to bitch and moan and complain and question whatever the fuck she wanted, whenever the fuck she wanted, and however the fuck she wanted, and his ass was just going to have to deal with it.

"Good," he kissed her neck and squeezed her. "Now I'm 'bout to shower and dip. Scramble me a couple eggs and some cheese grits right quick, bae, please."

Ambitious

Chapter Three

It was a little after seven o'clock when he walked into the Warm Springs Medical Center and was shown to Dr. Dean Thomas' office. After only a few moments of listening to the doctor speak, Killa politely interrupted him. "I'm sorry, doc. I hear ya, but look, I really ain't tryin' to hear that shit, no disrespect. I need to see Mileena and then maybe my mind will be able to make a lil sense of what you talkin' 'bout."

Nodding, Dr. Thomas smiled slightly and agreed. "Sure, I understand," he said and stood up from his desk. "Follow me if you will, sir." He led the way to Leena's room in silence and knocked on the heavy wooden door once they arrived. When a muffled response was called from inside the room, the doctor opened the door and peeked inside. "Good morning again, Ms. Wright," he said as he stepped further into the room. "There's someone here to see you."

Killa stepped into the room right behind the doctor and his heart skipped a few beats when he laid eyes on Leena sitting up in her bed. "Hey, baby," he said with a smile.

Leena fixed him with a blank stare for a few seconds before she kicked the covers off of her and swung her feet over the side of the bed. Wincing slightly, she scooted forward until her little feet dropped to the floor, and then, using the bed to steady herself, she began to amble slowly towards Killa.

By the time she reached him, tears had welled in her eyes, turning them to pools of clear green liquid, and just as she stepped into his outstretched arms, they fell. She cried tears of immense joy in his embrace as he gently squeezed and rocked her.

He leaned back just enough to look down into her face, and when he did so, she slowly wiped at his tears. He kissed her forehead and pulled her back into his embrace. "I love you. I love you so fuckin' much. I swear to fuckin' god I love you, bae," he whispered in her ear as she closed her eyes and relished being in the safety of Killa's arms again.

***

Killa closed the door to Leena's room, where she lay sleeping soundly, and checked the time. It was 8:22 a.m. "Listen, doc, I gotta go, but I mean, what I do? I mean, how I know when I can bring her home?"

"Well, assuming that all of the tests we run on her come back with good results, which I personally believe they will, it should only be a day or two, tops, before she's discharged. At which time, someone here will contact you, informing you that your fiancée is cleared to…"

Killa's gut wrenched as the doctor kept talking but his mind somehow blocked it out. The only thing he could think about was his fiancée, Leena. But what about Tiara? Amazingly, and as hard as it may be to believe, that was the first time that he'd even thought about his old dilemma. What about Tiara? His family, Doonie and the daughter he was expecting in the next month or so? What would he tell Leena if he stayed with Tiara like he wanted to? Or what on earth could he possibly tell Tiara if he left her and Doonie while she was pregnant to go back to his life with Leena, like he also, and maybe even a little more, wanted to do? The urge to fart pressed upon him and he let one out silently as his nerves and raw fear got the best of him. It took for the doctor to stop speaking and fan the air in front of his face with his hand to bring Killa back to earth.

"Whew," the doctor said while still fanning. "Mr. James, are you alright?" he asked, his face and ears turning a rosy red.

"Yeah, I'm good, doc. I gotta go. But listen, I'll be waitin' on the call to come get her," he said and quickly made his way out of the office.

"Yeah, sure," Dr. Thomas waved him out hastily. "Whatever. We'll be in touch," he said while pulling out a can of air freshener.

***

Vega disconnected the call and sighed heavily, thinking about the conversation he'd just had and the best way to handle this latest situation. Clipping the tip of one of his $94 dollar cigars, he looked over at the naked backside of the little Puerto Rican woman asleep in his bed. "Maria," he said and struck a wooden match, but the little lady didn't budge. "Maria," he called again, and a little louder. That time she began to stir. "Mamacita..." he spoke a short, rapid burst of Spanish that Maria immediately reacted to while he waved the match out.

She stood her four-foot ten-inch frame up and stretched before picking up her robe and heading towards the bathroom.

"Mamacita?" he said to her retreating back.

"Si papi?" She stopped and looked back at him over her shoulder.

"Leave the robe," he said in English. "I like to look at you naked."

Shaking her head, Maria giggled softly and dropped the robe right where she'd been standing before leaving the room.

Vega stared after her lustfully for a few seconds before snapping back to reality. How would he deal with this Chopper character? He'd always been somewhat weary of him whenever Brenton brought him around and now he knew why... because he was a piece of rat shit with no sense of loyalty or honor. *How could Brenton have missed that?* He thought to himself. And now, according to his connect inside the APD, his entire empire was running the risk of being destroyed by the piece of shit.

It wasn't too late to stop him, though, it was actually fairly early from an investigative stand point. He hadn't given the cock sucking police much to go on, so far. All he'd done was mention a few nicknames, Brenton's included, but it was clear to see that he was broken and ready to sing like a fucking canary whenever they came to him with a deal that he thought was worth selling his soul for. He took a long pull on his illegal cigar and placed a call to Miami.

"Yeah?" a deep voice answered in accented English.

"I need you in Atlanta tonight, Lobo," Vega said with cigar smoke coming from his mouth. "Don't worry about anything. Travel light and be ready to disappear when you're done here." He disconnected the call. Now, he had to call Brenton to discuss his piece of shit friend. He held the cigar in his mouth as he scrolled through his contacts and hit the *call* indicator.

***

Tiara checked the time on her phone and sucked her teeth. It was a quarter after nine a.m. and she hadn't heard a word from Killa since he'd left earlier. More angry with him than she was worried about him, she pouted as she flipped through the channels and gnawed on a cold drumstick. "Ol' stupid basta'd," she mumbled as she checked the time again. It was the same as it had been thirty-three seconds ago when she'd first looked. And then she had a thought. "Jo-Jo," she said aloud to herself.

Jo-Jo had been blackmailing her, threatening to reveal to Killa everything that he'd done for her if she didn't do little things for him. At first, it was cool because she would've done just about anything to keep Killa from finding out what she'd done, but lately, he had been asking for a little too much, too often. Like now, he was waiting on her to give him $4,500 dollars and just three weeks ago he'd told her he wanted $2,000 so he could buy a Louis Vuitton belt and pair of jeans.

Now, of course, she didn't have that kind of money, so the first time he'd demanded it, she exploded on him. "Where the fuck I'ma get that kinda money from, nigga?" she'd exclaimed.

Jo-Jo had shrugged his shoulders in a highly unconcerned manner. "All the blow yo' baby daddy movin' 'round the city, yo' ass better get it from him or some shit. I don't really care where it come from, as long as yo' ass get it, or I'ma start runnin' my damn mouth," he'd said with a smirk.

So then, just as she was about to do now, she took advantage of the opportunities Killa gave her to go in his little stash and take what she needed whenever he left her at home. She waddled to the closet in their bedroom and eased down to her knees. "Hmmph," she said, much preferring to be getting on her knees to steal a little money than to suck Jo-Jo's little ass dick. Her stomach turned and she scowled as anger burned through her body just from the thought of what his cold-hearted ass made her do.

One of the *little things* he had started out asking her to do was give him some pussy, which, although she hated it, was kind of okay because she could quickly get on him, fake a nut or two, and be done and on with her business in no time. But when his cold-blooded, evil ass found out that she was pregnant, he made a point of not asking for the pussy anymore, and even turning it down when she offered it. Instead, he wanted her mouth. And his dirty ass always made sure to skeet as much of his nut as possible in the most undesirable of places, like her mouth, eyes, hair, in her nose, ears, and wherever else he felt would annoy her the most. An uncomfortable chill worked its way down her spine as she recalled his slimy, stinky, semen in her mouth. "Ughhk," she said with a shiver as goosebumps covered her body, but she shook her head, along with the feeling, so she could handle her business.

Rummaging around in the closet, she located the right duffle bag and unzipped it. Quickly counting out the amount of cash she needed, and nothing more, she zipped the bag back and struggled to get back to her feet, grunting and panting the whole time.

Once again upright, she stood still to catch her breath, and while doing so, she heard the front door open and then close. "Baby?" she called out as she stashed the pilfered money away.

"What?" Killa answered rudely a few seconds before walking into the bedroom.

Tiara frowned. "Fuck wrong wit' you, nigga? What you got a attitude fa?"

"Nothin', I ain got no attitude. I'm just ti'ed as fuck."

"Well lay yo' big head ass down and rest then, boi, ain't nobody told yo' ass to be gettin' up at the crack of dawn leavin' the house anyway. We just fucked all damn night."

"I know right," he said and headed to the closet. "But I can't lay down now. I gotta dip right back out."

"What? You just got home!"

"I know, man, but I gotta go see my 'migo pahtna. I got some 9-1-1 shit from that nigga. Gotta go see what's up," he said and Tiara sighed deeply. "Don't start that shit, T, I swear I ain't in the mood," he said.

"I ain't even said shit, nigga, damn. At least let a bitch complain before yo' ass start accusin'."

Killa chuckled a little. "You right, bae, I'm sorry."

"Yeah, nigga, I bet yo' ass is," she snapped, causing him to frown.

"Man, whatever, wit' yo' smart mouth ass. I'm gone. I'll be back later." He headed out of the room.

"Don't come back, muthafucka."

"Don't tempt me, stupid ass girl, you know I won't," he called over his shoulder.

"Ya ass bet' not play, nigga. Be ya ass home at a decent hour, and you better damn call me." She trailed behind him ranting.

Killa just threw up his hand to acknowledge that he'd heard her as he exited their apartment, paying no attention to the door slam behind him or the deadbolt slide home.

***

He stared into space as he shook his head slowly. Never in a million years would he have ever thought that Chop, of all the muthafuckas in the world, would be the one to rat on him, but he'd heard it with his own two ears and seen it with his own two eyes. The news of Leena's awakening now seemed quite dull in comparison to this latest piece of information. Whoever Vega's connection in the APD was, he was obviously pretty high ranking. That's how he was able to get his hands on the tape of Chop's interrogation.

"So, my friend," Vega said and paused to dump the ashes from his cigar into a crystal ashtray. "The question is what do we do now?"

Killa had nothing to say. He was heartbroken and in extreme agony and pain at the moment. He honestly couldn't fucking believe Chop. He shrugged, and Vega took another puff of his cigar.

"Well, I have concocted a somewhat foolhardy plan with a good chance of success if it's executed perfectly. It's risky, but the possibility of it backfiring is slim. It will either accomplish what we need accomplished or it will not."

Killa nodded. "What ya got?"

"Let me get Brewster on the line first," he said, expelling a mouthful of cigar smoke as he fingered his phone.

Ambitious

Chapter Four

Killa drove in complete silence the whole way back to his apartment. His mind was occupied with thoughts of Leena and Tiara's sometimes annoying ass, but mostly of his pahtna, Chop. What in the fuck had his ungrateful ass been thinking? He was being taken care of like a fucking king, considering where he was. He never missed a week of commissary, two ho's from the hood phones plus the line to the trap spot on Linden stayed juiced up so he could call collect whenever he wasn't on the cell phone that he'd bought and sent to him. He was paying for his defense. What the fuck else could a nigga in the county jail possibly want? It was his own fault that he got banged up and nobody owed his ass a fucking dime, although the whole hood was fucking with him on the strength of the love they had for him.

Killa shook his head as he got out of his car and switched gears mentally, pushing Chop to the back of his mind and preparing himself to deal with Tiara. Apparently at some point during his extremely long morning, subconsciously, he'd began to think of her as being somewhat expendable now that Leena had returned, basically, back from the dead. Upon realization of this ludicrous train of thought, he cussed himself for being stupid and also verbally reminded himself that, not only did he love her black ass unconditionally, but that she was also Doonie's mother, pregnant with his daughter, and not to mention, he had just asked her to marry him not even twenty-four hours ago.

He sighed and stepped into the little apartment he shared with his small family. The sweet smells of potpourri and a lemon scented cleaning agent wafted to his nose. Nicki Minaj and Chris Brown's old hit *Right by My Side* played loudly from the sound system in the living room.

Tiara, in a pair of black Polo stretch pants, a white Polo maternity shirt, and barefoot, came waddling into the living room singing word for word with the music. "It ain't ya spit game," she smiled her beautiful smile and said when she saw that her man was home, clumsily dancing her way towards him. "It's ya dick game." She grabbed his hands and started an awkward looking two-step. "That got me walkin' 'round ready to wear ya big chain." Killa chuckled and flashed a grin that would make a woman's knees buckle. "I love you, baby," she said.

"I love you, too, shawdy," he responded, pulling her as close as her protruding belly would allow him to as he began to bop to the music.

She laughed, enjoying this rare occasion to see him at ease enough to actually be dancing. She kissed his lips and stepped out of his embrace. "What got you in such a good mood, Brent-Brent? You was mad as hell when you left earlia," she said as Nicki Minaj, Bobby V, and Lil Wayne's *Sex in the Lounge* started to play.

"Yo' ass was, too, but since you asked, you got me in a good mood."

"Awww, that's sweet." She batted her eyelashes playfully. "And I'm sorry, baby. I just be wantin' to spend some time wit' my suga-baby."

Killa laughed at her silliness. "I know, bae." He kissed her on the cheek.

"I'm hungry. All this cleanin' and shit got my damn stomach growlin'. You want somethin' to eat, baby?"

"Yeah, you," he said and groped her backside.

Tiara laughed and brushed his hand away. "Stop, boi, get you some rest. You know if you get me started, I'ma drain whatever energy you got left."

He squeezed her ass again. "I got a couple rounds in me," he drawled.

"Oh really?"

"Really," he said confidently.

"Ahhhh," she screamed out playfully in surprise and laughed as he, with the speed of a cat and with relative ease, scooped her off of her feet and carried her to their bedroom.

***

The dawning of a new day arrived quickly, a little too quickly if Chop had anything to say about it. He sat curled into a ball in a single man holding cell at the Fulton County Jail, absolutely livid about being awakened to go on a dry run. He didn't have a court appearance scheduled for another sixty-three days, so he knew that it was just a mistake, costing him a good night's sleep.

Keys jangled and rattled into the keyhole and then the cell door swung open and in stepped a yellow complexioned Sheriff's Deputy. "Johnson, Kelsey?" she said, reading from a piece of paper in one hand with a steaming cup of coffee in the other.

Chop took in her obscenely tight uniform pants before he looked up at her face. "Joy?" he said.

She looked up from the piece of paper and smiled, exposing two gold teeth, one on either side of her fronts, as recognition dawned on her face. "Chop? And you was the first person that came to my mind when I saw yo' name this mornin' but I swear I ain't think it would be you. Nigga, what's up? How you been, boy?"

"Maaaan, I ain't seen yo' ass in a long ass time."

"I know, right? We was still at Grady, wasn' we? Damn it's been a long time. How you been doin'? What you locked up fa? Please don't say murda," she said as her smile quickly turned to a seriously worried expression.

"Hell nah, man, you know I don't wanna do nothin' but get me a lil money. I got a lil dope case, shawdy."

She looked much relieved to hear that news from him. "Good. You know Tank and Quail was down here last week. Both of they ass got murda charges. Tank copped out to a life sentence."

Chop winced and shook his head at the misfortune of two of his pahtnas that he hadn't seen since his Grady High School days. "Damn, that's fucked up. Aye, what I'm goin' to court fa?"

"Uhhh." She looked back at the paper. "It say a bond hearin'."

"Bond hearin'? The fuck?" he muttered to himself.

"What? What's wrong?"

"Shit, really. I just didn' know. I ain't s'posed to go back to court for two mo' mont's."

"Well at least you goin' for bond. You might be able to get out. Who yo' judge is?"

Chop sucked his teeth and frowned. "Bitch ain't 'bout to give me no damn bond. I got Judge Shaw."

Joy looked at Chop like he was crazy. "Evon Shaw?" she asked.

Shaking his head, Chop said, "Hell yeah, man."

"Nigga, me and E cool as fuck. I'ma halla at her and get you a bond. Can you pay one? You need some help wit' it?"

"Hell nah, I'm good," he said excitedly. "I don't giva fuck how much it is, I can pay whatever if you can get her to give me one. I'll shoot ya somethin' if you get her to fuck wit' me."

Joy nodded. "Nah, boy, you know you good. You ain't gotta gimme shit. I'ma halla at her for ya."

"Hellll yeah, 'preciate it. I see yo' ass still hood as fuck," he said, smiling as he nodded his head.

Joy laughed. "You know what's goin' on, nigga, Edgewood, nigga, East Side shit."

Chop laughed and nodded his head again. She hadn't changed a bit. "Sho nuff," he drawled. "I wonda if that ass still fat," he said, dropping his gaze to her thighs.

She sucked her teeth and laughed. "Boy, yo' ass still the same," she said while shaking her head. "Look, I gotta go check on the girls. Somebody gon' be over here in a minute to get you

36

ready to go. I won't see you no mo' 'til we get to the courthouse, but I'ma make sure I halla at Shaw for ya. But listen, when you get out, hit a bitch up on Facebook or IG or somethin'. We can hook up."

Chop winced. "I don't really fuck wit' that social media shit, I don't even know how to work none of that shit. I be busy tryin' to get to the money."

"Nigga, just go on Facebook and type my name in." She tore off a piece of paper and handed it to him. "Queen of Joy," she said, handing him a pen also. "Write it down, and don't lose it. Queen of Joy. That's the name you type in and I'ma pop right up. Just send me a message lettin' me know you out and shit and I'ma hit you back. Gimme my pen back, crazy." She reached for it when Chop put it in his breast pocket. "You don't want them folks to catch you wit' that shit down there at the courthouse. Fuck 'round and be leavin' that bitch in a body bag."

Chop nodded and put the little slip of paper with her Facebook name on it in his breast pocket. "I got ya. I'ma hit ya up."

"A'ight. I'll talk to ya later," she said and turned around to give him a good look at her ass while she looked over the list in her hands before she walked out.

"Yeah, that mufucka still fat," he said to himself as he watched her say something to one of her fellow Sheriff's deputies and point at his cell. She knocked on his window and waved goodbye before she disappeared through a sliding door.

Chop nodded, sighed, and sat back down, silently praying that she really had the kind of pull that she claimed to have with *Lock 'em Up Shaw*.

***

"Okay, listen carefully to what I'm about to say because any deviation, or mishap, or whatever, is going to lead to you dying here today. Violently. Do you understand? Blink once for *yes*, twice for *no*."

The bound and gagged, middle aged, balding black man ever so carefully blinked his bulging eyes once to signal that he completely understood the set of instructions that he'd just been given. All but paralyzed by fear from being accosted in his home, his sanctuary, by this weird looking individual, he knew that he'd do right by understanding and complying with what he was told.

"I'm going to take this gag off of you now. If you scream or attempt to yell for help, you will die. Violently. Do you understand?" Another lone blink sealed the deal and off came the gag.

"Listen, brutha, we ain't rich but me and my wife got a lil nest egg we been savin' for the past twenty-eight years. It's yours, just please don't hurt nobody. I got my grandbabies upstairs. Me and my wife got them while one of our boys is on his honeymoon in the Bahamas. Please, just don't hurt nobody. Take what you want."

The weird looking, gun wielding intruder carefully sat down on the couch. "Are they twins?" he asked.

"Yes, twin girls," the bound man nodded eagerly and said, hoping that he and his family would be spared due to his willing cooperation.

"They're pretty little girls. I saw them while you and your wife were sleeping. How old are they?"

The bound man's mouth slowly dropped open and formed an O shape. The twins' crib was in he and his wife's bedroom, so if he'd seen them while he and his wife were asleep, then that meant that he'd been in their bedroom without them even knowing it. At that moment, even though he thought himself incapable of being anymore afraid than he already was, a little more fear gripped him. He shook his head slowly as terror shone in his glassy eyes. "Who are you? What do you want?"

"Who I am is not of any importance to you but what I want, and intend to get." He stood and reached in his pocket causing the bound man to squeeze his eyes shut, expecting to never open them again because death had overtaken him. "Is…"

***

Killa was up at the crack of dawn, again. This time he had an obscenely large bowl of Reese's Puffs cereal with almond milk in front of him and the television turned to one of the local news stations. Visions of Leena had peppered his dreams, and she even worked her way into his sleepy, conscious thoughts now. He couldn't fucking wait to get that call from the center telling him that she was ready to be discharged. But even though he felt like a kid that didn't know any better waiting on Christmas, sadly, he hated to admit that he had bigger fish to fry right now, and his name was Chop.

He switched the television from news station to news station, hoping to not hear about anything interesting as minutes turned into hours passing by. Eventually, after checking his phone for a missed call for the thousandth time, he dozed off to sleep right there on the living room couch at around 8:50 a.m. or so.

***

Two sharp knocks sounded at the door. "Come in," Judge Evon Shaw called from behind her desk. The door to her chambers opened and in stepped her bailiff, Deputy Joy Daniels.

"Hey, supawoman, how you doin' this mornin'?"

Judge Shaw smiled, genuinely happy to see her much younger friend/confidant. "Good morning, young lady, what's up? We got a docket full today. You ready to work?" she asked, picking up her steaming coffee mug.

Joy frowned and plopped down on the sofa beside the judge's desk. "Ughhk... I guess."

The judge laughed. "You shouldn't frown like that, sweetie, your face might get stuck like that."

Joy laughed at the little joke. "Judge, you know you my role model, right?"

"Ouch," she said after she burned her lip with her coffee. Grateful that it hadn't been her tongue or the roof of her mouth, she fixed Joy with a motherly stare. "What is it that you want, darling daughter of mine?"

"Well, I kinda, sorta, want you to do me a favor," she said slowly.

"Is it illegal?" the judge questioned.

Joy thought about it for a second before she answered. "Uhhh, I don't think the actual thing that I want you to do is. But me askin' you to do it prob'ly, more than likely is," she grimaced slightly.

"Ha," the judge said playfully with a sly little grin. "I'm listening, what is it?"

"Welllll, I kinda got a old friend comin' in front of you today and I was wonderin' if maybe you could give him a bond?" she asked, hoping that the judge gave her some play.

"A bond? Talk about anticlimactic," she said with a small frown. "That's it?"

"Well, yeah, I guess. I mean..."

"What kind of case is it?" she cut Joy off before she could ask for more.

"Drugs."

Nodding, the judge asked, "Is he eligible for bond?"

"I think so, he's..."

"Who is he?"

"His name Kelsey Johnson," Joy said eagerly and hopefully.

The judge stopped looking through her docket roster. "Oh, I know him."

"You do?"

"Yeah. Tall, skinny, Wiz Khalifa looking guy." Joy smiled. "I guess he is kind of handsome, if you're into the thug type. You sweet on him?"

Blushing, Joy nodded. "I guess. He took me to senior prom and he was my first."

"Oh wow," Judge Shaw said and punched a few keys on her keyboard. Looking at her computer screen, she said, "This guy has gotta be like the OG thug of the thugs," she joked as she looked at Chop's criminal history. "I've seen him at least once a year for the past, uhh, twelve years. Ha," she laughed, but when she saw the look on Joy's face, she quickly sobered up. "Why haven't I already granted him a bond, though?" she said more so to herself than to Joy as she punched a few more keys. "Oh that's right," she snapped her fingers. "Couple of guys from APD asked me to hold him for them."

"What? Why?" Joy asked, devastated. Her dislike of the APD was beginning to rise.

"Don't know, but sorry, kiddo, they don't want me to cut him loose."

"And you gotta listen to them? It ain't nothin' you can do?"

Judge Shaw shook her head slowly. "I guess I could but it just wouldn't look good. Sorry, sweetie, I wish I could do this for you," she said with a pained expression on her face. She really looked at Joy like the daughter she didn't have but had always longed for, so to see her sad and heartbroken really did hurt her. Her secretary buzzed her then. "What is it, Asha?" she said into the little speaker box on her desk.

"Steve's on line one," came the secretary's reply.

The judge picked up her phone and hit the blinking line. "Hey, honey," she said and paused. "No, what's wrong, is it one of the girls?" She paused and listened again. "Okay, hang on a second." She moved the phone away from her mouth but still hit the mute button. To Joy, she said, "Can you give me a second please? One of my granddaughters has probably wet her diaper and my husband seems to think that it's the end of the world," she said while rolling her eyes.

Joy giggled sadly. "Yeah, I'll see ya in a minute, anyway, it's 'bout that time," she said, eyeing the clock that was hanging on the wall.

"Right. Never get married, darling." She rolled her eyes again. "And maybe we can discuss bond for this gangster that you're head over heels about over lunch. I'll be sure to see him this afternoon."

"Okay," Joy beamed and quickly left the office, closing the door behind her.

"Okay, Steve, what's the problem?"

***

"Eve, honey, I want you to listen closely to what I'm saying and do exactly as I tell you," Steve said slowly before his wife of close to thirty years cut him off.

"Steven, I'm working and you're..."

"Baby..."

"Calling me pretending to have some kind..."

"Eve!"

"Of emergency, this is not the time to be goofing around..."

"Got-damnit, Evon Denise Shaw! Will you please just shut the fuck up and listen to me, got-damnit? For once, just be the fuck quiet and listen to your fucking husband without interrupting or talking back!"

Completely shocked at the language he'd just used, Judge Shaw gasped and shut her mouth.

When Steve heard his wife's silence, he knew he had her attention, so he began to speak in a calmer tone. "What I'm about to tell you, Evon, no one can ever know or find out. You can't say a word to anyone. Just listen to me and do what I ask you to do. No questions, no back talk, just do what I ask. Alright?"

"Alright," she agreed, her heart beating fast in anticipation.

"Okay, a man broke into our home this morning..."

Worry slammed into Evon like a freight train. "Oh god," she said, covering her mouth with one hand. "Are you alright, honey? Are the twins okay? Have you called the police?" she fired question after question rapidly.

"Evon! Be quiet and listen. Don't interrupt me again. Just listen to what I'm saying, understand?"

Taken aback, she frowned but dared not to defy her husband. She knew by his tone that he meant business. "Alright," she spat out.

"Early this morning, sometime while you and I were asleep, a man broke into our home and hid out. He waited for you to leave for work before knocking me unconscious and tying me up. This man is still in our home. I am still tied up."

"Oh my god," Evon whispered.

"At this very moment, the barrel of a gun is being pressed against the side of my head and the barrel of another gun is only a few inches away from one of the twins' face. This man has given me two things, a set of instructions to relay to you, and his assurance that if you grant his request, no harm will come to neither myself nor the girls."

"What? What is it? Anything. What does he want?" Judge Shaw urgently whispered into the phone because fear had all but snatched away her ability to speak entirely.

"There should be a man coming before you today by the name of..." Steven paused and Evon heard another man in the background murmur something indistinct. "His name will be Kelsey Johnson." The judge's heart skipped a beat when she heard the name again. "Evon, all that this man asks is that this Kelsey Johnson person be given a bond. He doesn't want the case dismissed, or dead docketed, or anything. Just give the guy a bond. Simple. Sweetheart, you can save my life and the twins just by allowing this man to bond out. Do you understand?"

Nodding, Judge Shaw whispered, "Yes."

"Honey, I'm not ready to die, and I don't want the twins to die either. Please, baby, our lives are in your hands."

Just then a knock sounded at the door to her chambers. "Don't come in. I'm busy," Judge Shaw cleared her throat and shouted.

"It's that time Judge," Joy's voice penetrated through the wooden door. "Everybody waitin' on ya."

"Let 'em wait, I'll be out in a minute."

"Good morning, Judge," a male's deep, accented voice came through the phone into the judge's ear. "I take it that you understood your husband clearly?"

"Yes," she responded as tears brimmed in her eyes.

"And are you going to comply with my wishes?"

"Yes."

"Good. Also, I would like to inform you that, should you notify the authorities, they will only find dead bodies, your granddaughters', your husband's, and mine, upon their arrival to your beautiful home. I assure you that I will not hesitate. I will not think twice. Do as I wish, leave the police out of this, and you have my word that life will return right back to normal for you and your family, and you will never hear from me again. Call your husband for more instructions when bond has been set for Mr. Johnson."

And just like that, the line went dead, leaving Judge Evon Shaw holding the telephone to her ear, blinking back tears.

Chapter Five

"All rise."

"Be seated," Judge Shaw said when she entered her courtroom and took her seat. "Bailiff?" she motioned for her Bailiff to approach the bench.

"What's up, bosslady?" Joy whispered quietly once she was close enough to not be overheard.

"Have another deputy fill in as my Bailiff and go wait for me in my chambers," she said without even looking at her.

"Okaaaay," Joy responded, kind of surprised. "Somethin' wrong?"

"No. Just do as I asked, please," the judge replied curtly.

Bewildered, Joy nodded and walked away. She beckoned for one of the other three deputies in the courtroom, and after a quiet, quick exchange of words, she was gone.

"Anthony," Judge Shaw said to the prosecutor. "There's a case on the docket that I'd like to handle first. I'm tired of seeing it, Kelsey Johnson. Deputy, could you have Mr. Johnson brought in please." The deputy she addressed nodded and left, returning quickly with a cuffed and county blued Chop. "Good morning, Mr. Johnson, you can be seated," she said as she flipped through a few papers. "Uhhh, this is a bond hearing, wait," she looked up. "Where's your lawyer?" she asked and glanced over at the prosecutor's table. They all shrugged and made other gestures that conveyed the fact that they didn't know.

Chop inhaled through his nose while sucking his teeth and shaking his head slowly. "I don't know where that dude at, man," he said while frowning. "I ain't even know I had no bond hearin' today. He ain't told me nothin'."

"How long have you been locked up, sir?" she asked him.

"'Bout seven mont's, judge," he replied.

"Okay, if the state doesn't object, I'm going to grant bond. State?" Judge Shaw said and looked over at the prosecutor's table.

Chop scowled because he knew, without a shadow of a doubt, that the judge knew that the cocksuckers were going to object. It was their fucking job to fucking object!

"Yes, judge, the state is opposed to bond being granted. Mr. Johnson is not only a repeat offender but we believe him to be a flight risk. Also, I believe there is some kind of law enforcement hold on him as well so, yes, Your Honor, we do not believe that bond should be set."

At that moment Chop, had the urge to wrap both of his hands around Judge Shaw's and the prosecutor's necks and choke the living shit out of both of their asses, but instead, he did the most rational thing his mind could come up with at the time. He sat back in his chair and shook his head in disgust with a deep frown on his face.

Judge Shaw punched a few keys on her keyboard. "I don't see any type of hold in my records, but either way, even the police can't override the law."

The prosecutor nodded. "Okay Your Honor, but there's still the issue of him potentially being a flight risk."

"Well, I think that he's been held long enough without bond for this type of charge, and as for him being a flight risk, I seem to think otherwise. Over the years, I've never had that problem out of him, but all the same, if he doesn't show for court, then a warrant will be issued for his arrest and our fugitive squad will have another fugitive to apprehend. Mr. Johnson?"

"Yes, ma'am?" Chop answered, stunned with disbelief at the turn of events. *Got-damn, Joy,* he thought to himself.

"Can you post bond?"

"It depend on how much it is."

"Well can you tell me what kind of bond you can post today, or as soon as possible?" she said while shooting a warning glance over to the prosecutor's table. They were obviously highly upset with her decision to grant bond.

Chop thought about his response for a second before he answered. "I can prob'ly do somethin' like twenny-five hunnid today. More than that might take a few weeks."

"Okay, you know what, don't worry about it," Judge Shaw said while glaring at the griping prosecutors. "I'll grant you a signature bond. I'm tired of this case. Signature bond has been set. Have a nice day, Mr. Johnson," she said just to spite the disrespectful prosecutors, and then tapped her gavel twice, signaling that the hearing was over.

As Chop was being led out of the courtroom, he heard Judge Shaw say that she needed a fifteen minute recess.

***

Taking off her robe as she entered her chambers, Judge Shaw walked in on Joy staring at the screen of her phone. "What're you doing?" she demanded.

"Postin' a tweet," she said with her smile quickly fading to a worried, curious expression as she showed the judge her phone. "Somethin' wrong? Whats goin' on?" she asked.

Settling into the chair behind her desk, Judge Shaw looked into Joy's eyes. "What's going on between you and Kelsey Johnson?"

Joy relaxed visibly and blushed a little. "Nothin' yet," she said with a shy smile. "I saw him at the jail this mornin' and we talked a lil. He told me you was his judge and I told him was go talk to you to try and get him a bond."

"That's it?"

"I think. Like, what you tryin' to know?" she asked, sensing that something was wrong.

A few tense seconds of staring into Joy's eyes in search of the truth or any signs that maybe she was lying or hiding something, and she looked away, satisfied with the conclusion that she wasn't involved with what was happening to her family. "Nothing. I just saw him. I gave him a signature bond."

Joy smiled. "For real!?" she asked excitedly.

Because of the situation with her family, Judge Evon Shaw, mother of two sets of twin boys, grandmother to seven, smiled, but only halfheartedly. Nodding, she said, "Yes. I took a quick recess, maybe you could say a few quick words to him before we start back. Hurry." She shooed Joy away with a smile still on her face.

Beaming with excitement, she was beside herself. "Thanks, bosslady," she said, and rushed from the room.

Sighing, The Judge picked up the phone and dialed her husband's number.

***

"Damn, nigga, you would rather sleep on the couch than in the bed wit' me? It's 'cause I'm fat, ain't it?" Tiara woke Killa up by saying.

"Go 'head on wit' that lame ass shit, T. What time it is?" he asked groggily.

She laughed. "I'm just playin', it's 12:18. I'ma spit this lil dime piece out and be back to my dime piece self in a few weeks, watch. Then I ain't go be able to pay yo' ass to stay outta bed wit' me." She laughed again and waddled into the kitchen.

When she came back, she had a Pop-Tart in one hand and her keys in the other. Killa was in the middle of checking his phone for missed calls. "Where you 'bout to go?" he asked.

"To halla at mama and get Doonie."

He frowned. "Get who?"

"Doonie."

48

"Who the fuck is Doonie?"

"Doonie, nigga, our son."

"We got a son?" Killa asked with an amazed look on his face.

Tiara laughed. "Yeah right, nigga, mama say she ti'ed of his bad ass. She want me to come get him when he get outta school today."

Killa laughed, too. "Man," he said wistfully. "It been so quiet 'round here wit'out that lil muthafucka scootin' 'round and gettin' into shit. We might need to leave his ass over there. Just pack up and move. Don't tell ya mama shit, stop answerin' her calls and everything."

Tiara laughed again. "No hell we ain't. I'ma go get my baby."

"I thought I was yo' baby?"

"You ain't shit, nigga, Doon-Doon my baby." She pulled a few of his dreads and kissed his cheek. "Anyway, I love ya, suga-foot. I'll be back later."

"Love you, too," Killa said as she walked out of the door. Yawning, he scratched his head and flicked some dandruff from under his fingernail. "I need to wash this shit," he mumbled, scratching his head again. When he stood up, his phone rang and he answered without looking at the display. "Yeah?" he said and listened quietly. It was time.

**

Reek stepped into his dormitory, 7-North-400, and as soon as he did, Rico spotted him. "Roommate, boiiii, what's up, boiiii? What them cracka's did for ya, bruh?" he asked as he approached and dapped his cellmate up.

Reek smiled. "This shit over wit', shawdy. The judge dead-docketed that shit."

Rico nodded. "That's right, too, I told ya that shit was some bullshit. Ain't no way in the fuck that shit was go hold up in court. So when you dippin'?"

Happy as hell to be getting out, Reek shrugged. "Shiiit, I ain't got no holds or nothin' on me, right, so I guess whenever these folks decide to let me out this mufucka."

Nodding again, Rico started to walk with Reek to their cell. "It'll prob'ly be 'round six or seven, that's 'round the time they been lettin' mufuckas out lately. Shiiit, my nigga, you know I'm s'posed to be gettin' out this bitch next mont', right?"

"Hell yeah, ya pahtna s'posed to be freein' ya, right?"

"Hell yeah, OG go fuck wit' me. But look, right, I'm tryin' to fuck wit' you, bruh. Le's collaborate on gettin' to this paypa when I get out this mufucka. Just gimme ya numba and I'ma hit ya line when I touch down and we can go from there."

"That sound 'bout right," Reek said while nodding. "I'ma make sure I shoot it to ya before I dip. And I'ma put 'bout two hunnid on ya books before I leave this mufucka, too. I fuck wit' ya, bruh, the long way."

"Check that," Rico said, but he wouldn't really believe it until he had a money receipt in his hand.

Reek sucked his teeth and stopped walking abruptly. "Awww, man. You know my pahtna I be tellin' ya 'bout? Chop?"

Rico nodded. "Yeah, what up?"

"That fool went to court today, too. They gave shawdy a bond, so he 'bout to get out, too."

"Sho nuff."

"Hell yeah."

"So y'all niggas 'bout to be back out there together."

Reek smiled. "Yeahhh, man, back in that ol' four finga no thumb spot, man, Boulevard, Linden Ave, Parkway shit. Real city shit, man. City life or ya bitch life," he blurted out happily and laughed.

Rico laughed with him and dapped him up again. "That's right, my nigga. Don't forget to gimme ya numba, man."

"Bruh, c'mo, man, le's go on and do it now just to make sure I don't forget homie." They started towards their cell again. "I'ma be lookin' for ya to hit my line."

"Oh, I'm most definitely go halla at ya, bruh, for real," Rico said as he entered their cell behind Reek and pulled the door up behind them.

***

Killa took the quickest shower in the history of humanity, and was dressed and behind the wheel of his trusty 442 in no time. As he pulled out of the apartment complex, he passed by his cousin Vito, who was driving the newest model Camaro.

He hit the horn twice to grab Killa's attention and shot him a bird when he looked before smashing the gas pedal causing the Camaro to fishtail for a second before catching a grip and shooting into the complex.

"Lame ass, nigga." Killa shook his head and mumbled to himself as he turned onto Covington Highway. He ate the pavement up as he raced towards Gwinnett County and Leena, but as fast as he moved, his mind seemed to be doubling his physical speed. He pulled into the Warm Springs Medical Center and parked, his heart thundering and his pulse quickening with every step he took after getting out of the car.

Upon entering the facility, he stated his business to the attendant at the front desk and was waved on back. Leena's room door was slightly ajar and he knocked softly before entering. "Hey, babe," he said.

She looked up from where she sat, tying her shoe, and smiled shyly. "Hey."

He gave the room a sweeping glance and settled his gaze back on her. "You ready? You got all ya stuff together?"

She nodded. "Yeah, I got everyt'ing," she said while pointing at the two bags sitting by the door. "I'ma call for dee docta. He said he wants to see me before I leave."

"A'ight." Killa smiled and went to sit beside her on the bed.

She'd already hit the call button so she cuddled up closely to him and rested her head against his shoulder. He kissed her forehead and smoothed her reddish brown hair, but neither of them spoke a word. The doctor arrived very shortly, and after some quick medical advice, he officially discharged Mileena Wright from his and his employer's care.

Killa had Leena wait under the elaborately built awning with her things while he went to get the car. She heard the familiar roar of the engine and dual pipes before she saw the black Cutlass pull under the awning. He had the top down, and instead of opening the door to get out, he hopped over it and went for her bags. Smiling at all of the memories seeing the old car evoked, she stood rooted to the spot, feeling extremely blessed to be there.

"What you smilin' at?" he asked.

She looked at him as he closed the trunk and nodded towards the car. "I see you're still driving dis."

He winked at her, his quick wit deciding to show its face. "Ain't no way in the hell I can ever get rid of this car, all the shit me and you done did in it." He chuckled and Leena's face turned fire engine red as she recalled some of the things that he was possibly speaking about. He opened the door for her to get in and then quickly made his way around to the driver's side door. Up, over, and into the driver's seat he went, but he didn't crank the car up. Instead, he looked over into Lena's beautiful, blushing face and smiled. "I love you, bae. I fuckin' missed yo' ass so fuckin' much."

"I love you, too, Brenton," she said quietly with a smile. He leaned over and she gave him a quick, passionate kiss.

"Now, where to, love?"

She thought for a second. "I don't know. But, I want some King Fish and plantain, and some peas and rice, and some coco bread," she said dreamily.

Killa nodded with a laugh. "You wanna go to Stuff Jerk?"

"Stuff Jerk?" She questioned.

"You know, that lil Caribbean restaurant you used to love on Memorial Drive." She shook her head very slowly, failing to recall what he was talking about. "Don't worry 'bout it," he said, cranking up the Cutlass. "You go fall in love wit' the spot all over again when we get there."

She nodded and smiled. "Good, and while we eat, you can tell me everyt'ing dat I've missed dese past what, nine, ten mont's."

Killa nodded and hit the radio. Future, Nicki Minaj, and Rick Ross' *I Wanna Be With You* began to pump from the speakers of the car as he pulled from under the awning into the sunny afternoon.

***

"You ever thought about bein' a porn star, shawdy?" Jo-Jo asked as he watched the video of her sucking his dick on his phone.

"What, nigga?" she frowned and said.

Ignoring her, he laughed. "This my favorite part right here. Yeah, bitch, drank that nut, nasty ass bitch, swalla all that shit," he said to himself, but loud enough for Tiara to hear.

Scowling, she jumped up from where she sat on the bed. "Fuck you, ol' stupid ass, lame ass nigga. Erase that shit," she demanded.

"Man, I ain't erasin' shit, this mine."

"Nigga erase it or I'ma go home and tell my baby daddy everything. He go kill me but at least I'ma die happy knowin' he go kill yo' bitch ass, too."

Jo-Jo sobered up. "I'ma erase this shit, but lemme tell you somethin', that nigga might scare the hell out of yo' ass, but he ain't shit to me. My gun smoke just like his. I'll wack his ass and not think nothin' else 'bout it, so remember that shit the next time you wanna threaten me." He made a show of erasing the little video that he'd made.

"Whatever, nigga. You erased it?" she snapped.

"Done."

"I'm 'bout to go."

"I'll be in touch," Jo-Jo said and snickered.

Tiara sighed. "Every day, I pray that you die in yo' sleep, or get hit by a bus while you crossin' the street or somethin'..."

He laughed. "You shouldn't be so negative, shawdy, god don't like ugly."

"I'm hopin' he make an exception in this case," she said and left the apartment.

Chapter Six

Killa and Leena were in the middle of their meal when his phone rang. He glanced at the display, saw that it was Tiara, and silenced the ringing. When she called back a few moments later, the fact that she was pregnant crossed his mind and he quickly excused himself from the table.

The fact that he'd answered several calls at the table already but then felt the need to excuse himself to answer that one piqued Leena's interest and she spoke on it when he returned not even a minute later. "Everyt'ing okay?" she asked.

He smiled. "Yeah, everything cool."

Nodding, she spoke again. "Now, are you ready to tell me everyt'ing I've missed and what's going on now?"

Somehow her tone of voice and the expression on her face conveyed exactly what she meant so he took a deep steadying breath before he began to speak. "For a while after you got shot, nobody thought you was go make it. Me, none of the doctas, nobody. Yo' dad had got at me and asked me to just let whatever was gonna happen, happen. So I waited, not really expectin' you to bounce back, shit, you had got shot in the fuckin' head, but still, holdin' hope that you would. After you had been in the coma 'bout a mont' or two, I started back fuckin' wit' Tiara," he said slowly.

Crushed, Leena's green eyes misted over, but she refused to cry.

"Baby, you was gone for a long ass time. I was lonely as hell and wasn't tryin' to be fuckin' wit' random ass bitches. You couldn't have possibly been expectin' me to wait almost a whole year wit'out knowing when or even if you ever would shake the coma."

Leena smiled a sad smile through her watery eyes. "I undastand," she said sadly while nodding slowly. "What else do you need to tell me? What else do I need to know?"

"She 'bout seven mont's pregnant now, that was her that just called, and that's why I got up from the table to answer."

Unable to take the last blow, she dropped her head and watched her tears fall to her lap. Killa got up and slid back into the booth on her side. He put his arm around her shoulders and pulled her close to him.

"I'm sorry, baby. I swear I am. I ain't know what to do, Leena. You was in the hospital, expected not to make it, and there she and Doonie was, so much history and familiarity already right there for me when I was in so much fuckin' pain over losin' you and our baby."

At the mention of the life she'd been carrying in her own womb the night she'd been shot, she sobbed harder.

"It's cool now, though, bae, everything go' be a'ight now."

After a few minutes, Leena got control of herself enough to speak again. "Well, here I am now, so where do me and you, we, go from here?" She looked up into his eyes and asked earnestly.

Killa took a slow, deep breath and stopped rocking, but he continued to hold her in his arms. The question, although a simple one, one that he'd constantly been asking himself recently, completely stumped him. He had no answer to it as he looked into Leena's beautiful face.

***

Chop picked the phone up and was right in the middle of placing the collect call when he heard his name called over the PA system in his housing unit. Wondering what the CO could possibly want, he hung up the phone and walked over to the button.

"You called Kelsey Johnson, man?" he asked the guard in the tower through the little intercom built into the wall.

"Yeah, pack ya shit, you just made bond," the male CO replied.

Chop frowned. "What? Made bond? I just got back," he said unbelievingly.

"Yeah. Yo' name Kelsey Johnson, ain't it?"

"Yeah."

"Well roll ya shit up, dog, you just made bond."

"A'ight," Chop said, confused as hell, though. Nobody knew he'd even gone to court today, much less been granted bond. Hell, he'd just been about to call the block and let somebody know to get word to Killa or Bam or somebody to come get him, but he didn't get a chance to.

Frowning as he walked slowly back to his cell, he wondered what the hell was going on, and then it hit him. "Joy," he exclaimed with a snap of his fingers. A big smile spread across his face and he hurried the rest of the way to his cell.

In under five minutes, he had everything that he was taking home from Rice Street, and twenty minutes after that, he was heading through release, happy as a muthafucka as he looked through a door with a plexiglass window labeled *Intake* at the niggas unfortunate enough to be getting booked into the county jail. "'Bout damn time," he mumbled to himself as he shook his head slowly and went to have a seat to await the release process.

***

"What's wrong?" Leena asked.

Killa glanced at his phone to check the time and sighed quietly. He'd been so submersed in his thoughts about his Leena/Tiara dilemma that he hadn't even noticed Leena standing in the doorway watching him for the past few minutes. "Nothin'." He shook his head. "You sure you wanna stay here, shawdy? You don't wanna go home?" he asked, glancing around the $1,900 a night suite at the Westin Hotel in the heart of Downtown Atlanta.

"I don't have a home anymore," she said sadly, her real meaning going over his head. He took it that she was talking about her house in Austell, but in all actuality, she was speaking about his heart. As she'd intended, he didn't quite catch on and she kept speaking. "I don't want to step anudda foot into dat house again until it's time for me to pack up all my t'ings and move out. Dis will work for dee rest of dee day. I'ma get a new place tomorrow."

An extremely awkward silence settled over the two of them, and had it not been for Killa's phone ringing, things probably would've gotten even more awkward. "Hello?" he gladly answered. "What?" he frowned and said after a few seconds of listening. "Listen, I'm 'bout to call you right back, just gimme a second," he said and hung up. He looked at Leena and started to say something but she cut him off.

"Go on, I undastand. You got a family now."

Her words, along with the look on her face, cut him to the bone. "It ain't even like that," he started to explain. But she threw her hands up, palms out.

"It's okay, I undastand. I'll be here 'til tomorrow and I have your numba. Go on and handle your business."

Killa shook his head, but didn't attempt to speak again. Instead, he kissed her cheek and reluctantly left the suite. Once he'd gained a grip, he took out his phone and dialed Vega back, who answered on the first ring, and they jumped straight to the business at hand. "Now what you was sayin', man?" he asked with a slight frown.

Vega's accented voice came through the phone slow and clear. "It seems that our friend has disappeared. Somehow he was able to bond out on something called a sign bond and disappear before my man could pick him up. You wouldn't happen to know anything about that, would you?"

Absolutely livid at what Vega may have been insinuating, Killa had to move the phone away from his face to keep from blowing on him, and in turn, possibly ruining their relationship. Before he brought the phone back to his ear, he realized that he'd actually stopped walking, so as he began his stride once more, he raised the phone. "Nah, man, you know I don't know nothin' 'bout no shit like that. But just be cool, I'll find him. He don't know what's goin' on 'bout his bond situation so he'a turn up soon."

"And when he does?"

"I got this shit, man," Killa assured him.

"Good. Now, Mileena..."

***

"Man, who the fuck that is, man? I know damn well that ain't my mufuckin' pahtna walkin' down this mufuckin' street man," Bam said loudly as he stood up from sitting on the low brick wall in front of the trap spot on Linden Avenue.

He threw the Wing Street wing he'd just started on down and looked around for something to wipe his hands on. Finding nothing, he licked his fingers and then wiped them on his T-shirt as he started walking towards a smiling Chop. "What's up, bruh? When the fuck you got out nigga?"

By that time, all of the loud talking Bam was doing had grabbed other people's attention and made them look to see what all the fuss was about. The next thing Chop knew, he was surrounded by a crowd of his pahtnas and dapping them all up. "Where that nigga Killa at, bruh?" he asked.

"Last time I talked to bruh, him and Leena was somewhere in Decata eatin'."

Chop frowned slightly. "You mean him and Tiara," he corrected his lil pahtna.

"Aww, man," Bam exclaimed and bumped his open palm against his forehead. "Boi, Leena done shook back, shawdy. She just got released from the lil medical place today, bruh," he said excitedly.

Feeling a surge of even more happiness at the good news, Chop smiled. "You for real, bruh?"

Bam nodded. "Hell yeah," he drawled as he started to walk towards the apartment. "C'mo, man, let's go in the spot for a minute. I'ma call Killa and let him know you out. Why you ain't tell nobody?"

Chop shrugged his shoulders. "I ain't even know, my nigga. But look, I need you to do some shit on Facebook for me, though, man," he said as he, Bam, and a few other hustlers stepped into the trap spot.

***

"Yeah, well I gotta go. This prob'ly my nigga hittin' my line now. See ya later," Joy said and got behind the wheel of her 350Z. She rolled her eyes and shook her head at the lame ass nigga who'd just tried to holler at her, and then checked the flashing alert on her phone.

It was a message from Facebook, and by the time she finished reading it, she had a smile on her face the size of Texas. She immediately responded back, via Facebook, to Chop. After replying, she tossed her phone into the empty passenger seat with her purse and cranked up the little sports Nissan. "You might be on to somethin' wit' ol' Chop, Joy," she said happily to herself as she put the car in gear and started to exit the parking lot of the Fulton County Jail.

***

Killa parked in front of the trap spot on Linden Ave. and pulled out his phone. He brought up his call log and tapped the screen to place a call.

"Hello?" a kid answered after the first ring.

"What's up, big head, where ya mama at?"

"What's up, daddy," Doonie replied. "She in y'all room. You wanna talk to her?"

"Yeah, lemme halla at her."

"Maaaaa," he heard Doonie yell just as somebody knocked on his window.

When he looked up and saw Sherrelle, he clicked the passenger door unlocked and she opened it. With both of her hands on the roof of the car, she leaned inside. "What's up, cutie? What you doin' out here? Chop and them in there."

"I know, right. I just wanna halla at Tiara right quick to make sure she straight. What's up wit' you, though?"

"Shit. You know me, I'm tryin' to get it. I just came through to halla at the boy Chop for a minute. It's back to the basics now."

Killa nodded. "That's right, fuck wit' me, shawdy."

"You already know," Sherrelle said as she closed the door back and walked off.

"Uhh, who the fuck that was?" Tiara snapped.

"That was Sherrelle, relax. What's up, what y'all got goin' on?"

"Nothin' really, thinkin' 'bout what I wanna eat."

Killa chuckled.

"Fuck you, nigga," she said playfully.

"I ain't even say shit, why you..."

"You ain't gotta say nothin', nigga. Why I gotta keep tellin' yo' ass I know you better than you know yaself," she said, and Killa could hear her smiling.

He smiled himself and then said, "Look, bae, I might be out all night. I gotta handle some shit and I don't know if I'ma feel like drivin' all the way home after I'm done." The silence after he finished speaking was so complete that he looked at the call timer to see if it was still counting. It was. "T?" he said.

"What?" Her voice dripped with attitude.

"You heard what I said?"

"Yeah, I heard that bullshit," she complained.

"A'ight. I'ma call ya later to check on y'all. I love ya," he said quickly and hung up before she could even respond or start bitching. With that out of the way, he allowed his mind to focus on the task at hand.

Chapter Seven

August Alsina and Yo Gotti's old hit *Ghetto* played loudly from the speakers of Joy's little Nissan coupe as she turned onto Linden Avenue, pulled alongside the curb, and parked in front of a handsome dude with dreads getting out of an old black car. He paused to get a good look at her and she enjoyed the obvious look of approval on his face once he'd gotten an eye full. She knew she was a complete ten.

Joy flashed her pretty smile at the handsome stranger and waved. "Hey, what's up," she said. "I'm lookin' for Kelsey. You know him?"

Taking in her Sheriff's uniform and the pistol holstered at her waist, Killa didn't hesitate. "Nah, never heard of him," he said and got back into the car. He cranked up and was just about to cut the tires so he could pull away from the curb when Chop, Bam, Cat-Eyes, and some other hustlers came out of the spot. He watched through the windshield at the exchange between Chop and the Sheriff lady, the hug, the squeeze and caress of her plump ass, and then he relaxed because obviously he had missed something.

Turning the car off, he got out. "Aye, say, nigga," he called out as Bam and the other hustlers made their way over to the Cutlass.

Chop looked at Killa and smiled. "What's up, my nigga," he exclaimed as the two of them made their way towards each other.

When they were close enough, they dapped, and Killa pulled his pahtna, his ace, into a crushing embrace. "I love ya, my nigga," he released Chop and said, tears threatening to run from both of his eyes.

"I love you, too, bruh," Chop said and paused, not quite sure if it was his own guilt eating at him or if there was something about Killa's demeanor that didn't quite feel right. "What's up, man, you a'ight?" he asked.

Wiping under his eyes with back of his curled index finger, Killa responded, "Hell yeah, man. It's just two mufuckas that I love that been gone, man. Both of y'all back now, bruh. Shit crazy, man."

"Yeah, man. You know I done heard 'bout my girl, bruh. Where she at?" Chop said, looking over at the Cutlass expectantly.

"She ain't wit' me, right, but who this is you got wit' ya right here, bruh?" Killa said as he took a step back, pointed at the Sheriff lady, and gave her another quick glance over.

"Oh, this my lil pahtna, Joy. Me and shawdy went to Grady together and she helped me get this bond today. Say what's up to my pahtna, shawdy," Chop nudged her.

"He told me he ain't know who you was," Joy said.

"'Cause you the police and I ain't know who the hell you was," Killa said and chuckled.

"Oh, well, hey again."

"What's hap'nin? Chop, boi, I gotta tell ya, homie, you got ya a pretty one there, jones." Joy blushed and smiled.

Cat-Eyes crazy ass said, "When I came out the house and seen that fine mufucka, I-I-I," he stuttered a little as he closed his eyes and nodded his head quickly, "started hopin' she was comin' to serve a warrant on me."

Everybody that was standing around laughed and the crowd began to make its way back inside of the trap spot.

***

A couple of hours had passed and Chop had showered and took off with the fine ass Sheriff's deputy, Joy, a little while ago. Killa, Bam, Cat-Eyes, and some other hustlers were standing around kicking shit on Linden as the sun was going down, everybody except Killa was serving. He was in the middle of telling Bam how Leena seemed to be the same as she was before she'd gotten shot when a young nigga he knew only vaguely walked up.

"What's up wit' y'all boys, man? Bam, lemme halla at ya for a minute," Trayon said.

Irritated by the interruption, Bam told Killa to hold on a second before he stepped off a few paces to see what the fuck Trayon wanted. "What's up, bruh, you got that bread?" he questioned in a no bullshit tone.

Immediately feeling some type of way, Trayon unconsciously frowned a little. "Damn, shawdy, I'm comin' to talk some business and you already tryin' to handle a nigga like a peon."

"Guess that mean no, so what's up? I was kickin' shit wit' my comrade befor you interrupted a nigga."

Literally infuriated by the little nigga's arrogance, Trayon just stood there for a second as he contemplated punching his ass in the face. He wasn't sure if he could beat Bam or not, but he did know that he could definitely get a fair one with him. All of Bam's pahtnas were his too, so nobody would jump on him. He closed his eyes and shook his head quickly to clear his mind, though. *Not now,* he thought to himself. "Maaaan, look, I owe you that lil bread, right, so look, I wanna buy another deuce," he said and reached in his pocket pulling out two separate wads of money. "And give you two bands in counterfeit. I don't owe you but thirteen hunnid."

Bam frowned and shook his head. "Man, hell naw. You ain't get no counterfeit dope, I don't want no counterfeit money. That shit cause too many problems, bruh."

"Damn, bruh, it seem like you just determined to not fuck wit' a nigga. Man, you see a nigga fucked up, a nigga out here strugglin'."

"That shit sound personal, my nigga, and just so you know, I ain't obligated to fuck wit' ya, but I have. That's why I sold you that deuce the other day, that's why I ain't pushed the issue for real 'bout you payin' me, that's why I'm 'bout to let you leave now wit'out givin' me the real money you wanted to buy that deuce wit'. But I don't fuck wit' ya to let you tell it. I want my money," Bam said while shaking his head, and then walked back over to Killa.

"What's up wit' bruh?" he asked Bam as he played Angry Birds on his phone.

"Shit, that nigga owe me a lil change and just tried to gimme me some counterfeit for it."

Killa looked up from his phone just as one of the birds that he'd launched split into three and crashed into a stone and glass house, killing three pigs. "You ain't take that shit, right?"

"Hell naw, fuck 'round and have the Secret Service crawlin' all 'round this bitch. I told that fool to keep that shit."

Killa chuckled and pushed Bam playfully. "Look at you, lil nigga, tryin' to run shit 'round this mufucka."

"Yeah, yeah, yeah, I got this shit, big dog," he said arrogantly as he unconsciously straightened his back and stuck his chest out.

Killa laughed again and slipped his phone in his pocket. "I'm 'bout to skate, lil bruh. Y'all niggas be safe, shawdy," he said, dapping Bam before heading towards the Cutlass.

"Check that, fuck wit' meh, bruh."

Killa nodded, jumped behind the wheel, and sped off, promising himself that he would handle his business tomorrow. "Nigga ain't had no pussy in a minute," he reasoned aloud to himself. "But tomorrow, fa sho."

***

Leena opened the door to her suite and there he stood, dreads hanging loose and as handsome as ever. Once, her knight in shining armor, now, she didn't quite know what to call him. She sighed and leaned against the doorway, tilting her head to the side. Damn! She loved this nigga. "What do you want?" She closed her eyes and asked.

Killa slung a few dreads back out of his face. "Can I come in?" his voice pleaded with her.

Taking a second to consider if she'd let him in or not, she sighed again and slowly turned away from the door, allowing him to enter.

"Bae?" he said to her retreating back, but she ignored him. "Mileena?"

She spun around and gave him a look that would've turned a lesser man to stone. "What?" she answered icily.

Killa frowned. "Man, I don't giv-a-fuck 'bout all that ol' shit there," he said, referring to the attitude she was giving him. "We need to talk."

Put off, Leena rolled her neck, bared her fangs, and plunged. "Really? About what? You about to get..." She looked away and blinked back her tears as she swallowed the lump in her throat. "Married, remember? You got a kid on dee way. You a real family man now." All of the pent up hurt and pain that she'd been harboring within since he'd dropped bomb after bomb on her earlier was starting to surface. "Muddafucka, why are you even here? Dat bitch laid up pregnant and here you is wit' me. Why? Leave, nigga, bye!" Before she knew it, tears were streaming from her eyes and she was faintly lightheaded.

"Damn, shawdy, you for real just go blast a nigga wit'out even considerin' how I must have been feelin' 'bout what the fuck was goin' on."

"Nigga, you couldn't have been feelin' too much of no kind of way. You didn't wait but what, a mont', so you say, before you went crawling back to dat bitch and fucking got her pregnant. It's nice to know dat I was on your mind for a whole t'irty damn days before you kicked me to the curb."

If looks could kill, there aren't any if's, and's, or but's about it, Leena would've dropped dead, twice once she got a look at the contorted mask of fury that was Killa's face. "Bitch," he exclaimed, the pitch of his voice rising to expel the word. He was a million miles beyond infuriated, he was out of his mind with rage. He was on the brink of needing to be admitted. His eyes were slits that masked the majority of the fire that raged wildly in them.

In the blink of an eye, he was upon Leena and jacking her up by the front of her shirt. All of her anger and spunk of just a second ago was out of the window now, only to be replaced with sheer terror. She hoped like hell that he didn't hit her as she cringed and cowered in his grasp, the tips of her stubby little toes just barely scraping the floor every now and then. "Lemme tell you somethin', you lil muthafucka," he said coldly and tossed her, no matter how softly, it was still a toss, onto one of the plush couches in the suite. "Sit yo' lil ass down," he hissed as she landed, bounced, and scooted into the corner of the couch, the terrified wild eyed look of a trapped wild animal on her face.

"Bitch," he said again. "I done kilt a hunnid mufuckas behind what the fuck happened to you. I done lost pahtnas and everything, a fuckin' baby, yo' ass almost... Man, I was a hot ass second away from killin' my damn self, and you got the fuckin' audacity to sit yo' ass up here and insinuate that I wasn' fucked up. Bitch, I'm still fucked up! If yo' ass only knew a third." He held up his thumb and index finger and pinched them together close to her face. "Only this much of what the fuck I done been through since yo' ass got shot, ain't no fuckin' way you would be able to fix yo' mouth to say no dumb ass shit like that. Now shut all that punk ass cryin' and shit up and relax. I ain't go hurt you. And you know I love ya, but yo' ass 'bout to sit right here and listen to every aspect of what the fuck my life been like since you got shot, and then, only then, I want you to tell me you still feel like I wasn' fucked up over what happened to us." He sat down and started to talk in a slow, calmer voice.

***

"I 'preciate ya helpin' me get that bond. Them crackas really had a nigga in that mufucka faded, real shit, man," Chop said to Joy and nodded as he exhaled the potent gas smoke from his lungs.

Joy took a small sip from her glass of Remy and looked out over the railing of her condominium balcony before she looked back at Chop. "I'm just glad we bumped into each other again after all these damn years. Shit seem like forever since the last time I saw you."

"Yeah, it do." He ducked the blunt out and reached over to take the little clamp bow out of her hair. "Shake ya hair out for me," he said to her once he'd removed it. She shook her head, combed her fingers through her hair, and looked Chop in his eyes. Just standing there looking at the pretty, high yellow, thick ass bitch turned him on. "I like yo' hair down like that, shawdy," he said.

"You do?" she half whispered as she inched closer to him.

"Hell yeah, shit sexy as fuck." She leaned and Chop met her, locking lips with her for a second before he pulled away. "Now you know you 'bout to have to gimme some of that pussy, right?" he mumbled.

Joy giggled and grabbed his hand. "Not out here, though. C'mo," she said quietly and led him inside, through the dining room where their empty plates still sat on the table with the scraps of the dinner that she'd cooked still on them, straight to her bedroom.

She pushed Chop down on the bed and crawled on top of him. Her lips found his again and as he palmed and caressed her ass, she pulled at his shirt. Once she'd accomplished her goal of removing his shirt, she saw the tattoo of the big 4 on his muscled stomach, along with what had to be hundreds of tiny dollar signs. "I always used to love this tattoo," she said and kissed it before pulling her own shirt over her head.

Off came her sports bra and out spilled her modest B-cups. She rolled off of Chop so she could get out of her pants and panties and he could remove his pants and boxers. "You got a rubba, Kelsey?" she huffed out. And just like that, Chop reached to put his boxers back on.

"Hell naw," he muttered, devastated.

"I got some," she said and crawled across the bed to her nightstand. She tossed him a Magnum and said, "Get it up."

Five minutes later, she literally had a knee on either side of her head as Chop bunny hopped in the pussy. He pulled out and had her flip over so he could blast her ass from the back, but it was a mistake. He should've known he wasn't ready, but it was too late. When she lifted her head from the pillow and put both of her hands on the headboard to brace herself as she started to throw that big yellow ass back, Chop bussed instantly. She was in the middle of screaming for him to fuck her harder when he stopped all of a sudden.

"Why you stopped, nigga, what's wrong?" She panted as she looked back at him, loose strands of hair clinging to her sweat dampened face. And then she felt what was wrong. "Damn," she whined and pouted as she dropped her face into the pillows. "Already, Chop?" her muffled voice whined again as she disappointedly punched her pillow.

He shook his head. "Been a long time, man. I just got out."

Frustrated, she sat up and shook her head slowly. "I ain't even get mine and I ain't got no mo' damn condoms."

"You got some plastic wrap?"

"Nigga," she snapped and popped him. "I ain't 'bout to let you stick no fuckin' plastic wrap in me, you damn fool," she said, fighting as hard as she possibly could not to laugh at what he'd just suggested. They both just sat there in silence then, in the semi-darkness of her bedroom for a few minutes thinking, until finally, "Chop?" she said softly.

"Hell naw, Joy. I ain't go do it so don't even ask. The answer is N-O."

"Please, Chop, I'm horny as fuck. I just need to get off once."

Chop closed his eyes and and shook his head. "I ain't 'bout to lick that pussy, Joy. Yo' ass can forget that shit."

"I'll give you some..."

"Nope."

"Dirty basta'd," she mumbled to herself and the two of them sat in silence again until finally, after about ten minutes or so of nothing, she spoke again. "Can you get it up again?" she asked in a defeated tone.

"I'm twenty-seven, shawdy, not sixdy-seven. this mufucka could'a been back up."

Taking a deep breath, she climbed on top of him. "Listen, Chop, do not fuckin' nut in me. You hear me?" She said firmly while pointing a stiff index finger in his face.

"I got ya, just... be cool."

She mounted and began to pounce on him. When the dick began to get real good to her, she turned around so she could ride it backwards. She put her hands on his chest and leaned back as she worked that pussy, screaming out and digging her French tipped nails into his chest every time the dick slid into her. But what she didn't know, was that the pussy was feeling more and more like warm butter to ol' Chop every time it swallowed him until...

"Damn, nigga! I told yo' ass not to fuckin' nut in me!"

"I couldn't help it. That pussy fi', shawdy, I couldn't even talk."

Joy rolled her eyes. "Stupid ass nigga," she exploded in a whisper. "C'mo, hold my leg up like that," she ordered him with another roll of her eyes.

Chop wound up skeeting in the pussy five more times before the night was over for them.

Chapter Eight

Killa lay in bed with Leena snuggled up nice and comfortable against him, both of them fully clothed and counting sheep. After he'd given her the entire run-down of exactly what had transpired after she'd gotten shot, she softened tremendously towards him and eventually all of her anger dissipated, leaving only pain and frustration in its wake. But not at him, hell no. Her pain and frustration stemmed simply and solely from the hand that life had been so cruel to deal her, them. What had happened to her wasn't his fault and she believed him when he'd relayed to her how hurt and lonely he'd been.

"I just needed to have somebody around that I was already familiar wit'," he'd said as a few tears leaked from his eyes at the remembrance of his despair.

She'd come to see that treating him as if he'd done everything that he'd done with the intentions of hurting her was just as wrong and painful as the injustices that they both had already endured at the hands of Nico.

A loud whining baby, no, his phone ringing pulled her from her slumber first and then him.

"Hello?" he answerd it groggily, as heavy breathing sounded in his ear.

"I don't know," Tiara's panicked voice said before she took two deep breaths. "Where you at, or what you doin'." Two more quick breaths. "But I need you here." Two more breaths. "Now. This baby comin', Brenton."

Killa jumped up then, wide awake. "Hey. Wait a minute. Hold up," he shouted as he stood in one spot in a half crouch, the phone pressed to his ear, his head snapping from left to right frantically, looking for god knows what. "Don't panic, Tiara. Whatever you do, just don't panic."

"Muthafucka, it sound you the one panickin'," she snapped. "just get yo' ass here, and fast." She hung up the phone, knowing that it would make him hurry.

"Tiara 'bout to have the baby," he said to Leena, but the pained look on her face stopped him cold. "Damn, man, I'm sorry," he said slowly as he recalled how she said losing their child made her feel.

Smiling sadly, Leena shook her head. "No, don't be. You should get going. She needs you."

With a look on his face that told her how much he appreciated her understanding, he placed a tender kiss on her forehead and caressed her cheek. "I love you, Mileena."

"I love you, too, Brenton," she said back and he hurried out of the room. It was 5:17 a.m. and not even thirty seconds after he left, her tears began to fall.

***

At 2:51 that afternoon, July 30th, Tiara gave birth to a bundle of joy. Killa became the proud father of a healthy, beautiful baby girl that weighed six pounds and seven ounces. Tears of unfathomable joy sprang to his eyes when he held his daughter for the first time.

"Uh-uhn, baby, don't hold her like that," Tiara said, exhausted.

"I got her, Teet. Look at my lil princess," he said as he stared down into his daughters sleeping face. Wrapped in a pink blanket with a few thick, unruly curls peeking from underneath her little pink hat, Bianca Marche James was the most beautiful person on the planet right then. Black as an ace of spades, just like her mother, Killa couldn't stop smiling.

His deep baritone disturbed her, though, because as soon as he spoke, she started to wriggle and whimper in his arms. He shushed her and rocked her gently but it took for her to open her eyes and look up into her father's smiling face to be quiet. With a yawn, she blinked slowly and lazily a few times before closing them back to sleep.

"Bae," Killa hissed. "I ain't know her eyes was brown like that."

"Yeah, they hazel," Tiara said through a yawn of her own.

Killa shook his head slowly, already thinking of ways he was going to have to keep the little boys away from his princess. He had already decided that she would have to be at least thirty before she was even allowed to date, and that was nonnegotiable.

Doonie burst into the room then, making a ton of noise, followed by Ms. Tina, but Killa shushed them immediately. "She sleepin', y'all," he whispered to them.

In a lowered tone, Doonie walked over to his father and said, "Daddy, she my susta. Can I hold my susta?"

"Not yet, you might drop her," he said, just barely louder than a whisper.

"No, I ain't, I ain't go..." he frowned and protested loudly before remembering he was supposed to be keeping his voice low. "I ain't go drop her," he finished in a loud whisper.

"Uh-uhn," Killa said, thumping Doonie's forehead playfully before handing Bianca to Tiara and excusing himself from the room for a second.

***

Chop stepped out onto the porch of his trap spot and looked around. Damn, it felt good to be back. The day before, when he'd gotten out of the county, he was happy to be free again. But this was a completely different feeling now. Actually being back on the block with a bomb of work, in a fresh pair of True's, and a full day ahead of him to do what he loved to do more than anything else in the world, grind. There was absolutely no feeling that could even come close to matching it. He smiled and shook his head slowly as he walked out to the edge of the street.

Making his way up towards Parkway, he spotted one of his young pahtnas walking towards him. "What's up, young nigga?" he said with a smile.

"Maaaan, what the fuck up, big homie? What the fuck goin' on, fool?" Trayon said as he dapped Chop up.

"Coolin', bruh, what been goin' on?"

"Shiiit, big bruh," Trayon said slowly while rubbing his head. "Not a bitch ass thing, nigga been fucked up, shawdy, strugglin'. You know my lil brutha got that leukemia bullshit, right, been tryin' to help my mama and susta pay for his medicine and shit, man." He shook his head. "Shit been hard out here, bruh."

"Damn, bruh," Chop said with a wince. "I ain't even know Lil Chris was fucked up, man."

"Yeah, man, you was locked up when they diagnosed bruh."

"You need somethin', shawdy?"

Caught completely off guard, Trayon shook his head. "Shiiit, hell yeah," he said slowly. "Somethin' like what, though? What you talkin' 'bout?"

"Shiiit, my nigga, I can shoot ya a couple zips or somethin'. I ain't 'bout to give ya no paypa, but you can grind them and you don't owe me shit for 'em. Just come fuck wit' meh when ya catch up, my nigga."

"Hell yeah, my nigga, I'm wit' that. You already know I'ma fuck wit' ya. You the only mufucka 'round here that's fuckin' wit' a nigga."

"C'mo, bruh, real niggas do real shit." He dapped Trayon again. "C'mo down to the spot wit' me right quick so you can get this shit," he said as they started back down the street. When they walked into the apartment, Loose and Brandon, two hustlers from the hood, were still on the couch playing Madden. "Where Bam at?" Chop asked them.

"That fool in the back. What up, Tray?" Loose said as he juked a would-be tackler on the game with Devonte Freeman.

"What's hap'nin, bruh, what the score is, Brandon?" Trayon asked.

"Seventeen, seventeen. We in overtime now. I got this nigga ass, though," he said as he held his mouth open and moved his tongue around erratically while moving his whole body around with the controller. He was entirely into the game. "He 'bout to owe me, uh-oh. Three. Hunnid. Nigga," he jumped up and said three hundred just as he intercepted a Matt Ryan pass.

"Damn, man," Loose exclaimed as he dropped the controller and then dropped his head to his hands.

Chop laughed and headed to the back as Trayon took a seat on the couch.

Bam was putting his phone in his pocket when he walked into the room. "Tiara just had the baby, shawdy, she weighed almost seven pounds. Bruh 'bout to send some pictures of her now," he said with a smile on his face.

Chop smiled himself. "For real, bruh, where they at?"

"He say they 'bout to leave Grady in a minute."

"Awww, man, we gotta slide through there and check the baby," Chop said as he stared off into space for a second, thinking about the new baby. "I need a deuce of powda, man," he snapped out of it and said.

"A'ight, I'm 'bout to get it in a minute," Bam said as he pulled out his beeping phone.

"A'ight," Chop said, and left the room. "Killa girl just had the baby y'all," he said as he passed through the living room on his way to the kitchen.

"Everything good wit' her?" Loose asked.

"Yeah, I think everything straight. He ain't say shit 'bout that," he said as he bit into a cold slice of pizza.

"Here go this deuce, bruh. Killa sent some pictures of the baby. She cute as fuck, too, man," Bam said as he walked into the room with his phone in one hand and a zip-lock bag of cocaine in the other.

"Give that shit to Trayon, shawdy. Lemme see the pictures," he mumbled through a mouth full of pizza.

Bam frowned and looked from Chop to Trayon and then back to Chop while pointing in Trayon's direction. "Man, homes paid you for this shit?" he asked. Trayon just sighed and shook his head slowly, his expression turning sour.

"Nah, I'm 'bout to give it to him," Chop said nonchalantly.

Bam turned and looked Trayon in his eyes. "You got me fucked up, nigga, yeen gettin' shit. Yo' ass dead, boi," he scowled and said.

"You heard ya boss man, nigga, be a good lil worker-boy and gimme my shit," he goaded with a smirk on his face.

"Man, what the fuck goin' on wit' y'all niggas?" Chop said as he walked over towards them.

"I tell you what, nigga, how 'bout you get yo' bitch ass up outta here before I shoot yo' stupid ass," Bam warned, and as he did so, he put his phone in his pocket and sat the cocaine on the counter.

Loose and Brandon eased away from where Trayon was now standing, but Chop rushed the rest of the way over. He could look at Bam and see that things were quickly about to get out of hand if somebody didn't intervene. "Hold up, man. What the fuck y'all niggas got goin' on, man? Ain't 'bout to be none of that shit y'all talkin' 'bout in here."

"Naw, man, watch out, Chop, man. This nigga think that just 'cause niggas know he'a shoot somethin' everybody s'posed to be scared of him. I ain't scared of yo' ass, bruh, or none of ya pistols yo' ass be hidin' behind."

"Naw, nigga, yo' ass think that just 'cause yo' lil brutha sick everybody owe yo' ass somethin'. I'm obligated to take care of Tuna three lil girls, nigga, not you and yo' lil brutha. And for the record, bitch ass nigga, the Baby Bam-Bam don't hide behind shit. I don't need no pistol, nigga, I'ma fuckin' animal wit' my hands. I'll beat yo' mufuckin' ass, nigga."

"You got me fucked up, lil-bitty ass nigga. Gimme a head up then," he said arrogantly.

"Nah, man, y'all ain't 'bout to fight."

"Man, shut the fuck up, Chop, and stay the fuck out my video," Bam snapped as he yanked out his .40 cal and gave it to Loose. "I swear to god you ain't said shit, bitch, bring yo' ass out here to the street, fuck nigga," he said and marched right past Trayon, being sure to bump into him hard as he headed out of the apartment.

Trayon stood rooted to the spot with an apprehensive look on his face. He honestly hadn't been expecting Bam to take him up on his offer. He'd been all but sure that the little nigga was going to tuck his tail and run at the first sign of a fist fight with him, but somehow he should've fucking known better.

"Trayon, get yo' bitch ass out here, nigga. Aint no sense in tryin' to hide now, pussy. Yo' ass asked for this shit." They heard Bam call from outside. He looked and saw a crowd gathering quickly as Bam paced back and forth in the middle of the street.

"You heard that man, get on out there. Ain't no sense in pootin' and fartin' and shit now, you asked for that shit," Loose said with a grin.

Brandon laughed. "That lil nigga 'bout to beat yo' ass if you don't know what you doin', bruh. I been watchin' homes beat niggas since we used to be in Metro," (Fulton County Juvenile Center).

Chop just shook his head as the three of them followed Trayon out to the street. It was about to go down.

***

Vega smiled and shook his head. "It is good to finally see you up and healthy again, Mileena. Hopefully, you change you mind about business. Brenton just isn't bringing the kind of money we used make."

Leena smiled sadly. "I don't t'ink so. I'm done, Vega. I've made enough money for five lifetimes. I'm going to quit while I'm ahead. Maybe you should, too," she said, truly humbled by her life's experiences.

Vega closed his eyes and shook his head. "No, no, no. No such thing as enough for me, family business."

"Yeah, I know."

"Maybe you maybe help Brenton with people who buy. He seems to be stuck on two hundred kilos," he said and snickered.

Leena rolled her eyes and giggled. "I'll see what I can do."

Vega quickly sobered up and looked his friend of ten plus years in her beautiful eyes. "Goodbye, Mileena."

"Goodbye, Vega." They embraced and he placed a friendly kiss on her forehead before walking away. She closed the door to her suite and sighed. She'd decided to stay another day or two after Killa had rushed out earlier that morning and now, she wished like hell that he'd call or come over or something. She was lonely and missed him like crazy.

Sighing again, she turned the TV on and picked up the phone to order a little room service.

***

Jo-Jo hit the gas and then sipped from the double cup Double-D had poured up for him. "Stankin' ass bitch don't wanna act right, won't answer the phone and shit. I know this bitch see me fuckin' callin. I got somethin' for her ass," he said as he tapped the keyboard on his phone. When he reached the brink of no return, he stopped and zoned out as he stared at the screen. The blunt of gas was burning slowly in his fingers as the lean he'd been sipping all day, along with the Xanz and gas, fucked with his mental.

Snapping out of his zone after a few minutes, he tapped the screen of his phone again and shared the video with the world via You Tube, Facebook, and Instagram. "Punk ass bitch." He said and laughed as he brought the doubled up Styrofoam cups to his lips.

Ambitious

Chapter Nine

Killa disconnected the call and rubbed his eyes. Vega was more than right, he was exact. This shit needed to end. Now. Fuck everything else that was going on, this shit took precedence over it all. As much as he wanted to put it off, he no longer had a valid excuse to. Leena was cool, his daughter was here now, and he knew exactly where to find the nigga.

Shaking his head, he wished Vega's man hadn't fucked up now. He took a deep breath and walked into his bedroom. Tiara was sitting on the bed, Bianca asleep in her arms with Doonie peeking over her shoulder at his baby sister. "I gotta dip. I'll be back tomorra."

Tiara frowned. "What?" she said quietly.

"I'm 'bout to dip. I'll be back."

"Bye, Doonie," Tiara said, dismissing her son as she stood and put Bianca in the crib that Killa had assembled next to their bed. Doonie scooted out of the room and closed the door behind him. "Killa, I'm 'bout to ask you this shit one time and I want the fuckin' truth, nigga. What the fuck is really goin' on wit' you? Is you fuckin' cheatin' on me?" she asked calmly.

"No, I ain't cheatin', Tiara."

"Well answer this. What the fuck could possibly make you leave me alone, today of all days, talkin' 'bout you go be back tomorra? I don't understand this shit, Brenton. You told me not to trip but you doin' too fuckin' much now, for real."

"Just trust me, Tiara, damn. If you look back through our history together, you gon' see that I ain't the one that be fuckin' 'round."

"Nigga, what the fuck that s'posed to mean?" she raised her voice and said.

"Nothin' shawdy," he said, immediately regretting it as he stepped over to the crib and rubbed the back of his fingers against his daughters cheek. "Keep ya voice down, man, she sleep. Look, T, I ain't 'bout to fuckin' argue and fuss wit' yo' ass every time I need to leave the house, I'm grown. I'm takin' care of all my responsibilities. I'm yo' nigga. I'm yours. You got me, so just relax, man. I'm 'bout to leave and I'ma be back tomorra."

Tiara took a deep breath and looked away while shaking her head, and Killa took that opportunity to make a break for it. He kissed her and hit the door.

***

"Bruh, why you do that man like that? That lil nigga Chris already sick and shit, man."

"Man, fuck Trayon. Go get some mo' ice," Bam said, interrupting Loose. A lil freak from around the hood named Zora got up from where she'd been sitting on the couch beside him holding a bag of ice under his eye and went to the kitchen. "That was a statement ass whuppin for anybody else that might wanna try this shit. I don't play, shawdy. Plus, that bitch ass nigga asked for that shit, bruh," he finished as he worked his sore jaw. Trayon had caught him with a solid ass left hook that had kind of shaken him up a little.

"Yeah but you ain't have to do him like that, though, bruh. You embarrassed homes in front of the whole hood, man," Chop said.

"Fuck I was s'posed to do, big bruh, take it easy on that nigga and fuck 'round and get smashed? That nigga can fight, homes. And I ain't 'bout to wear no ass whuppin if I ain't got to, jones, I'm sorry."

"You s'posed to whup that nigga ass, look how much bigga he is than you," Zora said as she sat back down with fresh ice cubes in a sandwich bag. Bam reached for the bag but she swatted his hand away. "Watch out, boy, I got it," she whined.

"Nah, don't go out bad, but at the same time, shawdy, y'all niggas pahtnas, or at least y'all used to be. I know this for a fact. I remember I used to see y'all young niggas together all the time. But you just beat that man ass like he was a complete stranger or some shit, and in front of the whole hood," Chop shook his head. "That shit ain't right, bruh. You shouldn't have did that shit, cuz."

Loose nodded. "Yeah, you blasted that nigga. That nigga pride might not be able to stand up under that type of pressure. You a lil nigga, too," he said, wincing and shaking his head with a little laugh.

Nodding, Bam thought about what they were saying for a second, and then got a bright idea. He stood up. "Y'all right. Gimme my pistol, shawdy," he said to Loose.

"Don't give that nigga that strap, bruh," Chop said.

"Oh that nigga already know he dead. I ain't 'bout to give him no pistol so he can go shoot my pahtna wit' it," Loose said seriously while shaking his head, although he was smiling.

Zora was looking scared as hell by then. Fighting was cool, even she fought sometimes, but shooting people was a different story. She really was ready to get up and get the fuck on at that point.

Bam frowned. "Damn, but it's cool to let ya pahtna shoot me then, I guess," he said while shrugging. "Y'all was just talkin' 'bout the nigga pride and shit. What if he catch me down bad?"

"I ain't go let him shoot you neither. But you ain't go' shoot him."

Bam nodded and shrugged his shoulders. "I got a thousand guns, shawdy. You can have that one," he said and walked out of the apartment, heading to his spot to get another pistol.

Killa was pulling up just as he was stepping outside. "What's up, bruh, fuck happened to yo' face?" he asked as Bam walked towards him.

"Just got in a fight wit' that nigga Trayon." They dapped.

Killa frowned a little. "He beat ya up?"

An arrogant smirk came over Bam's face. "C'mo, man, I just spanked that baby. You know I don't fuckin' play, I'm just a lil bitty nigga."

"Damn sure don't look like it. What y'all fightin' 'bout?"

"Some bullshit, take me to the crib right quick."

"C'mo," Killa said as he got back in the car. "Chop in there?" he asked Bam when he got in, but just as he finished saying it, Chop and Loose came out of the apartment.

They walked over to the car and Loose gave Bam his pistol back. "Don't shoot that man, shawdy," he said.

"I ain't even thinkin' 'bout that nigga as long as he don't fuck wit' me."

"Where my god-daughter at, man? Congratulations, my nigga," Chop said.

Bam got out of the car, and when Killa did so, he and Chop dapped and hugged. A smile played at Killa's mouth, but his eyes were sad as hell. "She at the house wit' T. I got some pics of her, though," he said and fumbled in his pocket for his phone. Bam was already showing Loose the pictures Killa had sent him earlier.

Chop's excitement over the baby was contagious, and before long, he'd convinced Killa to take him out to his crib to see baby Bianca. "Nigga, I wanna see her. I wanna hold her, nigga. I want her to see me, and then after that, my nigga, I wanna go see my girl Leena." Killa nodded slowly, he could do that. That was the least that he could do. "I'm 'bout to go put this dope up and then I'ma be ready to ride," Chop said and bounded towards the apartment.

"I'ma ride wit' y'all, bruh," Bam said.

"Yeah, that's cool."

Loose yawned. "I'ma stay 'round here and get off some mo work. I'ma catch up wit' y'all niggas a lil later on. Congratulations, though, fool," he said and dapped Killa.

"'Preciate ya, homie."

Loose started to walk down towards Central Park Place.

"What's up, bruh, you good? Seem like you kinda down, my nigga," Bam said, looking at Killa.

"Nah, man, I'm good. Ti'ed as fuck, been up since like five this mornin' wit' Teet," he lied. "What's up wit' you an this nigga Trayon, man? And don't let me find out shawdy whupped yo' ass, bruh." He changed the subject and laughed as Chop locked up the apartment and made his way to the Cutlass.

***

"Doon-Doon, you seen my phone, honey?"

"Yeah, it's on the counter in the kitchen. I wanna go outside, ma."

Tiara yawned as she laid across the bed. She was tired as hell and needed some rest bad. She'd been up since before dawn. "Go get my phone for me," she said, and glanced at the little radio clock by their bed.

Doonie ran off and was back in a flash. "I think the battery dead, ma. You want me to plug it up?"

"Yeah, thank ya, baby," she said as she burrowed her head into her extremely soft pillows and closed her eyes.

Doonie plugged the phone to the charger next to the bed and just stood there. He wasn't sure if he should disturb his mother again, but he wanted to go outside bad as hell. He'd just seen some of his little friends walking by the apartment with a basketball.

After about thirty seconds or so, Tiara spoke. "Gone, Doonie, be back in the house before it get dark out there, and don't make me have to come find yo' ass like last time or I'ma whup yo' ass in front of all ya lil friends, includin' that lil nasty girl yo' ass be sneakin' and kissin' on."

Somehow, and he never understood how she did things like that, by the way, his mother just seemed to know things. She knew he was standing there still. He was staring straight at her face and he was positive that her eyes were closed but he just shrugged. "Okay, ma, I'ma be back on time." Some things were just too spooky to ponder on for long. He turned and left his mom and baby sister alone to sleep. It was time to play.

***

"Damn that shit crazy, my nigga, seein' her up and kickin' shit like that after what she done been through, my nigga. That's a blessin'. Straight up," Chop said as he, Bam, and Killa left the Westin after visiting Leena for a while.

Bam nodded. "Hell yeah. Somethin' seem a lil different 'bout her, though. She don't look the same or some shit," he said and shrugged his shoulders.

"She just a lil smaller, bruh. She gotta get her weight back up. That's all it is," Killa said as he headed back to 4th Ward.

Bam told him a little earlier that he would have to see the baby some other time, something had come up for him, so they were headed to drop him off and then out to Killa's spot.

***

He let himself and Chop into his apartment and silence greeted them. That seemed a little strange, but he didn't say anything. Turning on a light and the TV for Chop, he headed to the bedroom.

Tiara was stretched out across the bed on her stomach, knocked out, and when he stepped over to Bianca's crib, he saw that she too was asleep.

"Hey, baby," Tiara mumbled. She hadn't moved.

"Hey, mamabear, I thought you was sleep," Killa said lowly.

"I was."

"How you knew I was in here then?"

She laughed quietly. "I don't know, I just knew. She still sleepin'?"

Shaking his head at the apparent clairvoyance, he answered. "Yeah, she out like a light," he said and lightly rubbed her back. "How you feelin', T, you a'ight?"

Tiara sat up and scratched one of her titties. "Yeah, just ti'ed. I'm 'bout to get up, though."

"Where Doonie at, bae?" he asked and reached into the crib, picking up Bianca.

"I told him he could go outside," she glanced at the window." He should be back in a lil while. What you doin', baby? Let her sleep."

"I got her, T. Chop out there. He wanna see her." Bianca opened her eyes and whimpered and whined a little at being bothered, but hushed up the second she got comfortable in her father's arms. Tiara frowned at Killa's retreating back but didn't say anything. She loathed Chop. "She sleep, cuz, but here she go," he whispered loudly as he walked into the living room with his daughter. He handed her to Chop and looked on with sad eyes, unconsciously, as Chop cooed over the infant.

"She beautiful, dog. Congratulations, homie. You gotta make me god-fatha, bruh?" he turned expectant eyes to Killa.

"C'mo, man, you already know. Lemme take some pictures, shawdy." He pulled out his phone.

A little while later, after Chop had seen enough of the baby, he and Killa headed back out to the Cutlass. "I got some shit I wanna show ya, too, bruh," Killa said as he cranked up the car.

"What is it?" Chop asked.

"You go know when you see it, fool." He put the car in gear.

***

Tiara heard Killa leave and then went to use the bathroom. When she finished, she checked on Bianca and decided to share her little blessing with the world. Pulling out her iPad, she logged into her Facebook account. "Damn, I got a lot of inboxes. Mufuckas must already done heard," she said to herself and smiled as she opened the most recent inbox.

"Halla at me, shawdy. I need some of that!" The message from a nigga named Dixie Hill Red said.

She frowned. "Who the fuck is this lame ass nigga and what the fuck he talkin' 'bout?" she said aloud to herself with a shake of her head. Moving on, she read the next inbox from somebody named The Westside Ambassador.

It said, "Damn, Tiara. 404-246-3393 Hit my line ASAP! I swear I'll pay for it!"

"The fuck," she said as her frown deepened. The next message was from her friend, Ms. Best On The West Kiki.

It said, "Girl, what the fuck you got goin' on? Call me like, yesterday, bitch. Bye."

She inboxed Kiki and asked her what was up before checking out her page timeline.

A girl she knew from Oakland City named Baby Tinky had posted on her timeline and by the time she'd finished reading it, she was smoldering with rage. She read the post again, and slower. It said, "Shout out to all the trifling ass bitches out there. Great job for letting this lame ass nigga record yo' stupid ass, and look! In case you didn't know, it's a baby in yo' stomach, nasty bitch, that's why it's all big and round like that, while yo' ass drinking and swallowing all that fucking come. SMDH! Making us look bad! #NASTYTRIFLINGASSBITCHES." The post had close to one hundred likes already and it had only been up for one minute. In a rage, Tiara did a little digging, and a few seconds later, she was looking at a clip of herself sucking Jo-Jo's dick.

90

She bolted up and ran to her phone, yanking the charger that was attached to it out of the plug. She had Jo-Jo's phone ringing almost as soon as her phone was in her hand.

***

Something didn't feel right. Why the fuck was he following Killa through the woods? Enough was enough, he couldn't take it anymore. "Bruh, what's up? Where the hell we goin'?" Chop stopped walking and asked.

"I guess right here," Killa turned and said sadly as he drew his .38 and pulled the hammer back.

The pistol leveled at his chest, Chop threw his hands up instinctively. "What you doin', man? Stop pointin' that shit at me, bruh."

"I trusted you, man. You my mufuckin' brutha, dog. How the fuck you go stab me in the back like that, bruh?" Killa said quietly.

"What the fuck you talkin' 'bout man?" Chop asked, his heart rate at two hundred beats per minute.

"I'd'a never thought in a million years you'a rat, my nigga," he shook his head and said, the revolver still pointing at Chop's chest.

"I ain't no damn rat, nigga. What the fuck you mean?"

At that moment, if he hadn't seen and heard it himself, he probably would've believed his pahtna, his homie, his brother. But that wasn't the case because he had. "Shut the fuck up lyin', bruh. Me and Vega seen the tape of yo' interrogation. How the fuck you think you got a bond all of a sudden?"

"You don't know what the fuck you talkin' 'bout. You and Vega ain't seen shit. Joy got me that bond. She know my judge, bruh."

While Chop was doing his best to explain himself, Killa was fumbling in his pocket with his free hand. He pulled out his phone and thumbed the screen a few times and then Chop's voice issued from the little speaker of the phone. It was the portion of the interrogation where he had named the nicknames of a few of his pahtnas and vowed that upon his release he could easily get real names to match the aliases. It seemed that he dropped his head a little lower with every name that he heard pass from his own mouth on the recording until he was finally staring down at his feet.

"That ain't you, bruh?" Killa asked, but Chop couldn't speak. "I'm sayin', my nigga, tell me right now that that ain't you talkin' and all this shit go be over and done wit'." All Chop could do was shake his head. "That's what I thought, my nigga. But why though, bruh? What mo' you wanted a nigga to do for ya?" he asked in an almost pleading tone of voice.

"I can't go to prison, Killa, man. You know that shit ain't for me, bruh," he mumbled.

"So you go turn ya pahtnas in so you can get off? Nigga, we ain't get caught. You did, bruh. That's some bullshit, Chop. That's some bullshit and you know it!"

For a few moments, only the sounds of crickets and other creeping insects and little critters in the woods was all to be heard. "Bruh, if y'all seen that whole interrogation then you know that what I told them folks ain't enough to do shit. They need me to tell them some mo'. That's why they ain't came and got nobody yet." Chop closed his eyes and shook his head. "Man, I swear to god, you let me go, my nigga, I ain't tellin' them folks shit, man. That's on everything, bruh, I'ma take my lick. Just let me go, bruh."

As much as he hated to, Killa shook his head. He thought about all of the murders that Chop knew they'd committed last summer and just couldn't risk letting him have the opportunity to save his own ass by turning him in for them. "You know I can't do that, Chop. You know I ain't go do that," he muttered as he repeatedly tightened and loosened his grip on the pistol.

"Don't do this shit, Killa, man. I just was holdin' ya daughta, shawdy. You just told me I was go be her god-fatha, bruh. How the fuck you go turn around and do some shit like this? I love ya, man," he pleaded with tears in his eyes.

"Nigga, how the fuck you love me when you was just tryin' to turn a nigga in to save ya own ass? You all in my face skinnin' and grinnin', mufucka, askin' to be my lil girl god-fatha an shit, but all the while knowin' you was 'bout to send a nigga to chaingang, nigga. You ain't shit, bruh. But I still love ya, shawdy."

"It wasn' like that, bruh," Chop started, but Killa looked away defiantly, a shaft of moonlight shining through the trees and reflecting off of the tear streaks on his face. "So what, you just go kill me, bruh?" he asked as he dropped to his knees slowly. "We ain't Nino Brown and G-Money, Killa. This ain't New Jack City, bruh. This shit for real. You do this shit and it's over wit' for good, homie. You really just go down bad ya pahtna like this? After all the shit we done been through together, bruh?" He looked up into Killa's eyes.

Killa took a deep steeling breath. "You right, Chop. This shit is real life, and in real life, real niggas don't rat on they pahtnas, bruh. I love ya, shawdy," he said and closed his eyes. He squeezed the trigger two quick times, and just like that, his ace was no more. Chop lay on his back in the woods, his open but unseeing eyes staring up at the night sky and treetops, two gaping wounds in his chest.

***

Tiara literally couldn't stop the tears from falling from her eyes. Jo-Jo had fucking snapped. He didn't care that she'd been at the hospital in labor all day, and he had refused to take the video off of the internet. He was doing his best to ruin her.

"It is what it is, shawdy. You wanna play, so I'ma play, too. I ain't takin' that shit down. Get over it," he'd told her and hung up after growing tired of talking to her about it.

The brightest spot in this grim, grim situation was that she knew Killa wasn't much of a social media guy. But while that alone might buy her some time, she knew that it wouldn't be much. Because of her own popularity throughout Atlanta, not to mention his, it would only be a matter of time before he got wind of the video.

She stopped crying for a second as her mind crunched a particular train of thought about how she could possibly salvage whatever she could from the inevitable catastrophe. When Killa saw the video, he was going to go ape shit. This she knew to be fact. Without a doubt, their relationship would crash and burn, newborn baby and all. But, if she was to tell him why the video was even able to be made in the first place, everything, from the beginning... "Bitch, hell naw," she hissed. There wasn't a doubt even the size of a mustard seed in her mind, body, or soul that the day she did such an idiotic thing would be the day that she left god's green earth. Shaking her head, she cringed at just the thought of what Killa might do to her if she told him what she'd done.

Her tears started again as she thought about her daunting situation. But she was only afforded the luxury of crying and contemplating in peace for a short period of time. Bianca had awakened and, more than likely, she was whining because it was time to eat. "Damn," she grumbled grimly.

***

Leena opened her door and there he stood, again, with the most pitiful looking expression on his face. And then he grabbed her. Pulling her close, he broke down. Moving into the room just enough to allow the door to close, Killa dropped to his knees, wrapped his arms around her waist, and buried his face in Leena's stomach, crying relentlessly.

She didn't know what was going on or what was wrong, and at the moment, she really didn't care. All she'd figured out was that Killa needed her and she was one hundred percent there for him. She moved some of his dreads and hugged him while patting and rubbing his back. She didn't speak, but one thought echoed repeatedly in her mind as she tried to keep herself from crying with him, *I got your back, baby.*

Ambitious

Chapter Ten

The next month passed with a haze over it for Killa. Chop's funeral had been a sad affair. A lot of who's who in the city had showed up to pay their respects, and Killa, who'd protected his pahtnas name and honor by not telling a single living soul about the treacherous act that he'd committed to cause his own demise, was comforted a little by seeing all the people that had love for Chop. Tiara had mysteriously come down with some kind of illness or another, "Some female shit," she'd claimed.

Angry beyond words at her lack of support for him, Killa just shrugged and went on about his business, assuming that it was just her passionate dislike of Chop that had prevented her from attending the funeral. Leena had shown up, though, hanging back mostly, not wanting to draw any attention to herself. She was still spooked about what had happened to her, and understandably so, but still, at least she had come. The Sheriff chick, Joy, and an older woman people were whispering was a judge, showed and left quickly as soon as the service was over. Doonie, the little handsome devil, cried quietly during the service. He was going to miss 'Unc Chop' while Bianca's beautiful little self was well behaved as usual, not bothering to cry even once as Killa held her. She was the talk of the hour, aside from Chop.

A good bit of the funeral's attendees had seen Tiara's infamous video, but everybody who hadn't assumed that Killa had already seen it also, had enough decency to not make mention of it at that gathering. He and Chop were notorious for being as thick as thieves, and everybody respected the fact that he was mourning the loss of his brother from another mother.

All of that had been about two weeks ago from the present day and time. At the moment, he was pulling into a set of gated condominiums in Atlantic Station. He parked his Mercedes C 300 coupe next to Leena's AMG, and since a lot of times he had a baby on board, he'd decided to upgrade from the Cutlass to something a bit safer, just to be prepared for an accident. He still had the Cutlass, but he'd sold Tiara's Acura and bought both of them Benz's. He'd also moved his little family into a subdivision of newly built townhouses out on Stone Mountain-Lithonia Road in Lithonia. He hated to move, but he had to admit, it provided a ton of much needed space for all of them.

Unbuckling his seatbelt, he got out of the car and opened the back door. With a smile, he shook his head. "What you been lookin' at back here, Princess?" he said as he got Bianca's car seat out. She looked at him attentively for a second before looking away and waving one of her arms, baby drool all over her chin. Killa chuckled. "What that s'posed to mean, lil lady? Leave you alone?" he asked as he threw the strap of her diaper bag over his shoulder and picked up her car seat.

Another beautiful, successful looking woman got on the elevator with him, and as usual, fell in love with Bianca instantly. He was starting to believe that women really couldn't resist a man with a cute baby by the time he got off the elevator. "You go get me in trouble, Bumble Bee," he said to his daughter before knocking on Leena's door. When she looked at him pointedly again and then looked away, he was starting to also believe that maybe his daughter was a little smarter than average.

"Hey handsome," Leena said when she opened the door. "Hey Beans," she exclaimed as she took the car seat from him, kissed him on the cheek, and headed for the couch.

Killa fixed himself a glass of water and stood in front of the floor to ceiling window and gazed out at the impressive Atlanta skyline for a few moments. Turning around, he saw Leena playing with his daughter, who had a serious looking deadpan expression on her face from the coddling she was enduring, and laughed.

"What?" Leena looked at him with excitement bubbling in her eyes. She adored Bianca. Too bad the feeling didn't seem to be mutual.

"Look how she lookin' at you, shawdy. She don't like you messin' wit' her."

"Whatever. How you know? She just a baby," she said to Killa while rolling her eyes before turning her attention back to the baby. "He don't know what he talking about, do he?" she cooed in baby talk as she called herself tickling Bianca.

Bianca then took it upon herself to do something that she rarely ever did, cry. She burst out in tears, wailing like a banshee.

Killa laughed again. "Told ya," he said. "Put her back in her car seat. She like bein' in there." Leena did so and Bianca immediately hushed up. When Killa saw the hint of a smile on his daughter's face, he laughed again. "She off the chain," he said, walking to the couch.

Feeling some type of way, Leena stood up. "I'm about to go take a showa, mean ass little girl."

He would swear that Bianca smiled again and that was why he laughed again as Leena walked away. "C'mo, bae, don't be like that. She just a baby."

Leena ignored him and went on about her business. Half an hour later, she returned, smelling of roses and wearing a pair of red tights and a wife beater. Her reddish brown hair was cut short and styled, and her green eyes shone like emeralds. A small scar was on the bridge of her slightly crooked nose from where she'd been hit with the pistol. Her feet were bare and, to Killa's delight, she had gained a lot of her old weight back in all the right places.

She ignored the lust filled look in his eyes as she sat on the couch, keeping Bianca and her car seat between them. "I talked to Vega. He wants me to help you," she said lowly, Bianca was dozing.

"Help me wit' what?"

She weighed her words. "He wants me to help you, uh, step it up a little."

Knowing that Vega hadn't been talking to her about what he thought she was talking about, he asked her, "Step what up?"

Seeing how he was responding, Leena had a good mind to say forget it, but she continued. "He wants you to get more cocaine from him," she said lowly, wincing slightly.

Killa frowned and shook his head. "And he told you that, why? Muthafucka ain't said shit to me 'bout it."

Leena shrugged. "I don't know, but I told him dat I would at least mention it to you. And now dat I have, I want to talk to you about somet'ing more important," she said and took a deep, steadying breath. "I'm tired of doing dis." She pointed back and forth between him and herself. "I don't like dis side bitch shit. You told me it was gonna change, go back to how it used to be, but so far not'ings changed. You gonna have to make dee choice Killa. Me, or go and be wit' her and let me go. I can't take dis for much longa. I'm sorry. I just can't." She looked him in his eyes and said.

Killa sighed and thought for a second, he was kind of blown at the way she'd just sprung the whole ultimatum shit on him. "Can I have a lil time to think?" he asked earnestly.

"No, I need to know now," she said with determination.

Jealousy and suspicion flamed up inside of Killa. "You tryin' to halla at another nigga or somethin'?" he asked in a deceptively cool tone.

"Somet'ing like dat, I met somebody and he asked me out," she lied through her teeth.

"Who is it?" he snapped.

"Don't matta."

Killa relaxed and smoothed Bianca's clothes. "You right, it don't. I'ma kill his ass if I find out, though," he mumbled.

"You not go do no'ting. What's it gonna be?"

"I need some time Leena, damn. You askin' me to leave my family, shawdy."

"One dat wasn't so big before I got shot," she shot back with a nod towards Bianca.

"But now it is. Please, man, just gimme a lil time. Please."

She sighed and nodded. "Okay."

"But in the meantime," Killa closed his eyes and shook his head. "Don't let me catch no pussy ass nigga down bad. I swear to fuckin' god I'ma shoot his ass in the fuckin' face. Yo' ass is mine, Leena," he sneered. With that said, he stood, got Bianca and her things together, and left the condo without another word.

***

"Rico McAllister, stand up, young man," Judge Bennet said from his seat on his bench. Rico stood slowly and looked directly at the grey haired black man. "Under normal circumstances, I would never allow a plea of this nature. But given the unthinkable amount of tragedy that you've suffered within the past year, I'll allow Mr. Clifton to assume responsibility and enter a guilty plea for all of the said charges and receive a sentence of natural life," the judge spoke slowly and clearly for the record, shooting a quick glance at Monk and his public defender, both of whom nodded in agreement. "I understand that you are aware that in order for this plea arrangement to be accepted, you'll have to enter a guilty plea to these lesser charges and accept five years' probation, one of which is to be intense probation. Any questions about this plea arrangement, young man?"

Rico cleared his throat. "No, sir."

Judge Bennet nodded slowly. "Alright, son, I'm going to read out your charges and I'll need for you to speak loud and clear when you enter your plea. Understood?"

"Yes, sir." Rico nodded.

"Alright. Count one. Possession of a..."

***

"Aye, look, big dog, I ain't go never forget what the fuck you just did for me, man," Rico said as he and Monk dapped and embraced in the holding tank at Rice Street. "I don't giva fuck what it is, bruh, all you gotta do is hit my line and I got ya, my nigga. I'ma send ya a check every week or two anyway, but if you need anything else, man, just hit me, bruh."

"C'mo, young soulja," Monk said. "I already know, man. I just don't want you to fade away after a few years, man. That's all I'm worryin' 'bout."

"Never, nigga. Never ever, man, not unless I'm dead or somethin'. I love ya, big homie. You ain't gotta worry 'bout shit long as I'm breathin', fool. That's on Summa Hill, bruh."

Monk nodded and rushed to leave the cell when the CO came calling for his side. He was already feeling kind of fucked up, and the sight of his young pahtna, knowing that in just a few short hours he would be a free man again while he geared his mind up to accept the fact that he would die in prison, hurt him to his heart. But he was glad that everything had worked out the way that they had planned for it to.

As he walked away, somebody banged on the plexiglass window of the tank, and when he turned to look back, his teary eyes saw Rico standing at the window saluting the realest nigga he'd ever been fortunate enough to lay his eyes on. He threw up Zone 3 and mouthed the words, "Real Summa Hill shit." And then Monk bent the corner, he was gone.

***

Killa stepped into his townhouse and none other than Tiara's favorite rapper/singer, Nicki Minaj, serenaded him. She, Lil Wayne, Future, and Birdman's old hit *Tap Out* was playing.

"Hey, baby." She met him in the living room and said, pecking him on the lips.

With a sigh, he sat Bianca's car seat on the couch. "What up, mamabear?"

"What's wrong, boo-boo?" she asked as she checked to see if a sleeping Bianca's diaper needed changing. It didn't.

"Ti'ed, man," he told the partial truth.

"Well guess what, I got a surprise for ya." She grabbed his hand and pulled him. "Grab her and put her in her crib," she said as she led the way to the nursery. "Go lay her down," she prodded him and headed to their bedroom.

Killa put Bumble Bee in her crib and, once he saw that she was undisturbed by the movement, he headed to their bedroom. *Tap Out* was still playing, although she had turned it down, but she was nowhere in sight. "Teet?" Killa called out as he kicked off his shoes and laid on the bed.

A few seconds later, Tiara stepped out of the bathroom in an aqua blue, two piece bathing suit. "What ya think of my new summa body?" She struck a few poses for him. Her black ass skin was glistening and he had to admit that her body had bounced back into shape like a rubber band. Her titties were still full, but they looked good. Her stomach and love handles were virtually nonexistent, and the way the bright, aqua blue bikini contrasted against her black ass skin, molding to and cupping that phat ass made him want to scream, but he didn't. In fact, he didn't say anything, his mouth and throat were too dry for him to utter a single word.

"What you think, baby?" Tiara whined, continuing to pose. "I been workin' hard to get my body back right for my boss." Killa sat up and scooted to the edge of the bed as she walked sexily over to him, being sure to put her pussy right in front of his face. When he gripped that ass and licked her belly button, she threw her head back and laughed. "Stop, boy, that shit tickle." She tried to get away but he had her locked in.

Knowing that she was about to let it go down for the first time since giving birth, she slid to her knees. Working his shorts down, Killa pulled his boxer briefs down and out jumped his pulsing dick. "Bow, there it go," she purred sexily as she grabbed his dick, eased it into her mouth, and sucked him until they both were burning with desire. Working on him with her hands, she looked up at him. "I want you to fuck the shit out this pussy, baby," she demanded in a whisper.

"It ain't been long enough, shawdy."

She stopped working her hands and closed her eyes while shaking her head. "Look, I'm ready. This pussy ready, daddy. I know it's go be a'ight."

His mind clouded because he hadn't had any pussy since she'd had Bianca. If she said the coota could take the pounding she knew he was going to give it, then he was all for it. He nodded and she smiled as she started to untie the strings to her bikini bottom, but he stopped her. "Nah, leave 'em on, bae, just slide 'em to the side." He grunted huskily and laid back, her saliva and his own pre-come glistening on his dick.

She smiled again and climbed on top of him. Sliding her bottoms to the side at her opening, she grabbed his throbbing dick and guided him into her heaven. A shiver worked its way up and down her spine from the feeling of him inside of her again, at last, and the anticipation of what she knew was to come. Pleased beyond measures when she started to work that pussy on his dick, causing him to moan like he was her bitch, she smiled and sped up her pace.

Killa was on cloud nine. No pussy he'd ever had could ever compare to the way Tiara's was gripping his pipe. He looked up at her sexy, black ass, titties bouncing as she smiled freakily at him and moaned from the pleasure he was giving her, and he knew then that he never wanted to ever be without her. Leena wanted him to leave her and all of this amazing pussy? That bitch was fucking crazy. If she was around, he probably would've slapped the shit out of her for even suggesting something so fucking stupid. He had just made up his mind. *Decision made.*

Ambitious

Chapter Eleven

Laid back in bed with Tiara snugged up against him, Killa felt nothing less than the boss that she proclaimed he was. Thinking about the decision he'd made in the heat of passion, he slowly convinced himself that it was the right one. Letting Leena go and staying with Tiara was what was best for the sake of his family. *She got another nigga already lined up anyway*, he thought to himself. He kissed Tiara and threw the covers off of himself. Her eyes greedily devoured his naked, muscled, and heavily tattooed body when he stood up and went into the master bathroom. After showering, he walked back into the bedroom, still naked and tempting Tiara's self-control. Taking out a fresh pair of boxer-briefs, he stepped into them and started to dress.

"Bam called while you was in the showa. He said he want you to call him when you get out."

"What I told you 'bout answerin' my phone, T? You know I don't like when you be doin' that shit. I don't be answerin' yours," he said while rubbing on his Polo deodorant.

"I only answered 'cause I knew who was callin' and you was in the showa."

Not responding to what she'd said, he continued to dress. "What you 'bout to do, bae?" he asked when he sat down to slip on his footies.

Tiara yawned. "I'ma take a bath and wash some clothes. I wanna put some new pictures of Bumble Bee on Instagram. Nothin' really."

He stepped into a new pair of Louis Vuitton kicks and walked over to the dresser. Reaching into one of the drawers, he pulled out a wad of cash. He counted off a couple thousand dollars and gave it to Tiara for a little spending money, just in case she wanted to go somewhere or something, and stuffed the rest of it in the pockets of his True's. "I want you to look and see if you can find us a nice lil hotel in Hawaii. Don't worry 'bout the price, whatever. When I get back tonight, I'ma look at it and see if I like it, too. I wanna do somethin' nice for ya birthday, Mamabear."

Smiling from ear to ear, Tiara didn't know what to say other than, "Okay."

"Where Doonie at, bae?" he asked with a frown and a snap of his fingers. He'd known something wasn't right all along but was just then able to put his finger on what it was.

"He been buggin' me and mama to let him go stay wit' her for a few days. He miss his lil friends over there. He so West Side," she rolled her eyes and said. "That's all his lil bad ass talk about, West Side this, West Side that, get on my damn nerves wit' that shit," she said with a laugh.

Killa shook his head. "That's sad, shawdy, that nigga seven. He bet' not never let me hear his ass sayin' that shit, send his lil ass to a fuckin' boardin' school in Canada some damn where," he said as he left the room.

Tiara laughed again and got up to lock the door behind him.

***

Rico was a free man. Broke as a muthafucka, but free. He had two things to his name, an excellent face card throughout the whole Zone 3, but especially so in the streets of Summer Hill, and a shit load of guns that he didn't know the exact location of at the moment, but it wouldn't be too hard to track them down.

He took a drag on his Newport as he stood in the middle of Martin Street, staring at his mother's house warily. A craving for the cocaine gripping him as he stared at the bullet riddled house that she hadn't even bothered to repair. He shook his head and hit the cigarette again. Tobacco would be his new cocaine since he'd promised himself that he wouldn't snort another gram unless his pahtna, Monk, was snorting with him.

Hitting the cigarette one last time before thumping the filter away, he walked up the ragged, weed strewn driveway, up the crumbling brick porch, and raised his fist to knock. The door swung open just as his knuckles would've rapped against it and there stood his mother, looking a hot ass mess. Although it had been eons since they'd seen eye to eye, Rico loved her dearly, so it hurt him to see her looking so gaunt and unhealthy. For anyone who ever wanted to know what losing two children within a six month span would do to you mentally and physically, all you had to do was take a look at Ms. Mary.

She looked at her son with hollow eyes, devoid of love. "I been watchin' you standin' out there in the middle of the street like a damn fool for the past five minutes," she croaked. "I was hopin' you wouldn't come over," she said as she quickly shuffled away from the front door.

Rico shook his head slowly and looked away, hurt. He wasn't in the mood for one of her verbal tongue lashings. It was high time to get everything out in the open and over with because, whether she liked it or not, he was all that she had left, and vice versa. "What you want me to do, mama. I'm fuckin' sorry for whatever it was I did to make you hate me."

"Shut up, boy. I don't hate you. I hate that you always up to no good. I hate that you always, ever since y'all was lil, used to pull Nic into yo' shit just 'cause he was yo' big brutha, but I don't hate you."

Rico shook his head. "That's what I'm talkin' 'bout, ma. Ever since we was lil, you ain't never treated me like Nico. That nigga couldn't do no wrong in yo' eyes. He was always innocent and I was always guilty and responsible for everything. I was always a liar and Nic's word was always law. If you had'a believed me just half the time when I used to tell you that stuff wasn' my fault, I prob'ly would'a turnt out to be a better son."

Ms. Mary hit him with an Oscar worthy deadpan stare. "You done whinin', Ricardo, shit. You sound like a damn sissy. Nic gone now. Trencia, too. I know it's all yo' fault 'cause somehow it always is."

Rico snapped then. He grabbed his mother's frail shoulders and shook her violently. "Stop fuckin' sayin' that shit, ma. Nico the reason behind all this shit. All I ever did was try to help his ass. I'm yo' son, too, ma. Please, man, just fuckin' believe me for once in yo' life when I tell you I ain't have nothin' to do wit' Nico and Trence gettin' kilt. That was all Nico fault," he shouted.

Feeling a little woozy from the shaking her baby boy had just given her, Ms. Mary looked at him with a terrified expression on her face. Tears filled her eyes and she started to sob.

Rico dropped his head and sighed. He felt like shit for taking his frustration out on her, knowing that she was having a hard time coping with all the pain and loss. Not sure if she would allow him to, he reached to hug her, and to his surprise, she did. Also to his surprise, it felt wonderful to hug his mom again. It had been at least twenty long years, he was sure, since the last time they'd hugged.

"You all I got Ricardo. You all I got left, baby. Please don't go rippin' and runnin' out there in them streets and get kilt. What happened to Nic and Trencia is done. It ain't nothin' you can do to bring them back. Just let it go, for me," she pleaded through her tears.

Rico didn't respond, though. He was too caught up in the feeling hugging his mother again gave him.

***

"So look, bruh, you sure y'all go be able to handle all this work?" Killa asked as he sat down on the couch in the trap spot.

Bam, who had moved back in and taken it over for good since Chop's funeral, was sitting on the other sofa looking at some porn on his tablet with Loose peeking over his shoulder. "I don't know, bruh," he said. "But I'ma damn sure try to move as much of that shit as I can. Tuna lil girls be wantin' the world, and now I got two spots to pay fa. Hell yeah, it's time to step it up a lil." He paused the porn, logged onto You Tube, and typed *Atlanta hood fights* into the search box before hitting search. "Le's see who done got they ass whupped lately," he said and laughed quietly.

Killa shook his head and laughed to himself at his pahtna, who was still just a kid at heart.

"Somebody told me you an Tray on YouTube. Put in *Atlanta Fourth Ward* fights, shawdy," Loose said.

"Stop bullshittin', man," Bam said as he quickly modified his search, a big ass Mad Hatter grin on his face.

"Bruh, you playin' and shit. You need to be focused on how we go move all this work, man."

"I got this shit, big dog. I'ma halla at Juan over there on Cleveland and a few other niggas, Brick and them, couple other niggas that's doin' a lil somethin', you know. Just chill, bruh, all you gotta do is lay it on me like you said you was go do and we go do the rest," Bam said confidently.

"Yeah, just get it here and we got the rest, big bruh," Loose said without taking his eyes off of the screen of Bam's tablet. "Put in *Atlanta Freaks*, bruh. You and Tray ain't on that shit," he said after seeing that no new fight videos had been added lately.

Bam looked at Killa and grinned. "Man, get this freaky ass nigga on somewhere, man," he said while laughing and punching *Atlanta Freaks* into the search box.

"Y'all young niggas retarded, man. Y'all ain't got nothin' else better to do?" Killa asked as he stood up.

"Nope," they said in unison as he tapped on one of the most viewed videos.

Killa smirked and shook his head. "I'm 'bout to dip, bruh. I'ma get at ya tomorrw and let ya know what's up wit' the movement."

"A'ight, just halla at me fool," Bam said, preoccupied with the tablet. Loose was the first to recognize Tiara but he wasn't too far behind. He frowned. "Aye, bruh, this Tiara on this video, man," he said.

"What you talkin' 'bout?" Killa asked as he stepped over to where his two pahtnas were. He stood over Bam's other shoulder, and sure enough, when he looked at the tablet, he saw Tiara going crazy on some nigga's dick. Taking come in all in her face and hair, swallowing, and worst of all, pregnant as fuck. His stomach turned violently, making him want to puke. "Who the fuck that is, man?" he muttered, an inferno building strength inside of him.

"I don't know, bruh," Bam said.

"It say some nigga named West Side Jo-Jo posted this shit, though," Loose said matter-of-factly.

Stankin' ass bitch! Pregnant wit' my mufuckin' baby. I'ma kill this bitch, Killa thought to himself. "How I get to that shit, bruh?" he asked in a forced calm as he pulled out his phone so one of his young gadget whiz pahtnas could show him how to bring the video up.

Loose brought it up and bookmarked it for him. With that done, he left the apartment without so much as a glance back.

***

Rico took his time walking down Georgia Avenue, a Newport burning slowly between his fingers. He'd just found out from his mom that all of his guns, along with the rest of his other possessions, had been taken by the people who owned the little rinky-dink monthly storage place on Candler Road. According to his mother, his brother's baby mama had refused to keep paying the monthly fee for *a nigga that's 'bout to get thrown under the jail*. He shook his head in disgust as he thought about all the shit he'd done for his niece out of the kindness of his heart.

He took a long pull on his cigarette just as a black, late modeled Grand Prix passed him by. He didn't recognize the car so brake lights, and then reverse lights, made his heart start to beat faster. He wasn't strapped, nor did he know who it was. He hit the cigarette again and blew the smoke out quickly.

"What's up, big gangsta? I thought yo' ass was gone, boi. When you got out?" a short, pudgy, red nigga named Bully said from the driver's seat of the Pontiac.

Rico relaxed and hit the Newport again. "Few hours ago, what's hap'nin."

"Shiiit," Bully said quietly and rubbed his fat hand across his thick waves. "Fucked up, 'bout ready to take somethin'."

Rico pinched at the hair growing from his chin. "That sound 'bout right." He nodded slowly.

Bully looked into Rico's eyes for a second before saying, "Get in, my nigga. Where you headed at?"

Rico opened the door and got in the passenger seat of the Pontiac. "I don't even know, my nigga," he said.

With a knowing nod of his head, Bully put the car in gear.

Ambitious

Chapter Twelve

By the time Killa made it all the way home, he'd calmed down a lot. He was just glad that he hadn't gotten around to going to see Leena and telling her that he'd decided to stay with his family. Getting out of the Benz and heading up the walkway, Tiara met him at the door with her beautiful smile on her face.

"Hey, suga-foot," she said before realizing from his facial expression that something was wrong. "What's the matta, baby?" she asked. Killa shook his head and smirked as he brushed by her on his way into the house.

Worried, she closed the door and followed him to their bedroom. She watched silently for a few moments as he went to the closet and pulled out two empty duffle bags before she spoke again. "Baby, what's wrong? What you doin'?"

He put the bags on their bed and pulled out his phone. He brought up the video and made it play just before handing her the phone.

She literally lost control of her bladder for a millisecond and pee'd in her panties just a little when she took one look at the image on the phone before she started trying to explain. "Baby," she began, but Killa held his hand up, silencing her.

"You pregnant wit' my fuckin' baby, Tiara. How the fuck you go be doin' some shit like..." he said in a deadly calm voice before letting his sentence trail off. He shook his head and started to stuff money and clothes into the bags.

"You ain't go let me explain, Brenton?"

Killa shooed her away. "Go 'head on wit' that shit, Tiara. Don't nobody wanna hear none of that bullshit you talkin' 'bout. That shit for the birds, shawdy. Aint no fuckin' explainin' this shit," he continued to pack his things.

"Brenton, just lemme..." she pleaded, but he cut her off again with a loud sigh.

I got a video of you suckin' some nigga dick on my phone. You lettin' the nigga bus' all in ya face and shit. You swallowin' nut, man," he sighed again and shook his head slowly. "And you pregnant wit' my fuckin' daughta. You ol' nasty, slut bucket ass bitch. I fuckin' hate you, shawdy. I hate that we even got kids together. Listen to me, man, I'm tellin' ya what god love, shawdy, we done. It's over wit'. Yo' ass can have this house, that fuckin' car, the ring, everything. Ain't no mo' me and you, from this day forward, ever again. If it ain't concernin' my kids, don't hit my line. I'm serious, Tiara. Me and you ain't got shit else to talk about ever again."

Tears began to flow from her eyes. "What you mean? So you just go' leave? Just like that? You go walk out on me? You go leave yo' kids like this?" she said with a little aggression through her tears.

Continuing to pack his things, Killa ignored her, causing her to spring into action. She rushed to her nightstand and pulled out her small pistol.

"Nigga, you got me fucked up. Yo' ass ain't 'bout to go no fuckin' where. You ain't 'bout to fuckin' leave me again. I need yo' ass, boy. You ain't leavin' me, Brenton."

Killa paused and looked at the small revolver she was pointing at him and then went back to packing his things.

"Oh, you don't think," Tiara said, frowning. "You think I'm playin'. I ain't fuckin' around, nigga. I done been through this shit for the last damn time." She cocked the little revolver. "If I can't have you then ain't nobody else can eitha."

Zipping up his bags and tossing them over his shoulder, he looked at Tiara defiantly, daring her to pull the trigger.

Click! The hammer fell and seemed to echo as it struck an empty cylinder. Remembering then that she never kept the gun loaded for Doonie's safety, all Tiara wanted to do was close her eyes and cry. But instead, she threw the gun on the bed and rushed to block the doorway. "I ain't movin', Brenton. You go have to beat me."

With pleasure, was the first thought to come to his mind when she made the statement, but then he thought better of it and sighed as he shook his head and turned towards the bathroom. She couldn't possibly block both exits, and when she realized his intentions, she knew she was beat so she moved aside.

"A'ight, muthafucka, go on and leave, but I'ma call the police."

Killa stopped in his tracks and looked at her. "You the one fucked up, Tiara, not me. But now you wanna get a nigga locked up for some shit you caused."

"You damn right, if that's how you wanna look at it."

Killa smirked again. "Whatever, I'm still leavin'." And with that said, he calmly left the house.

In a daze, Tiara walked to the living room windows and saw him toss his bags onto the backseat before he got in and backed out of their driveway. Her tears beginning only after the tail lights of his C-Class were out of sight.

***

"I done made my choice man," Killa said when Leena opened her door. August Alsina and Nicki Minaj's *No Love* was playing lowly from within her place.

"And?" she said expectantly.

"You go let me in or do I need to stay out here? You got that nigga in there?" he asked suspiciously, peeking over the top of her head into her condo for any signs of her mystery admirer.

"Whedda I let your ass in or not depends on what your decision is, and no, nobody's in here but me," she said as she closed the door up some to stop his prying eyes.

Killa nodded and reached down, he'd sat his bags beside her doorway, out of her immediate eyesight. He stood back up with both bags clutched in one hand and looked into her beautiful eyes. "I wanna be wit' you."

Leena smiled slowly as her heart soared with joy.

"But look," he continued, a serious expression on his face. "Before we go any further, this nigga you was tellin' me 'bout, I want his name." He held up the pinky finger of his free hand. "I want his address and phone numba." Up went his ring and middle finger, and from the looks of it, he still wasn't done.

Leena rolled her eyes and smiled. "Boy," she said and turned around. "Get in here. Ain't nobody but you."

***

Bully hit the blunt of high grade mid as he and Rico sat at a table chopping the goods they'd just took. It wasn't much, about eighteen thousand in cash, close to two and a half pounds of gas, and exactly thirty-six ounces of lean. "I been thinkin' 'bout what you told me earlier 'bout that nigga Monk. That was some real shit what that boi did for ya, my nigga. I ain't never heard of no shit like that, not wit' these ol' watered down ass niggas that's out here pollutin' the streets now. That's a real nigga, bruh. I salute that nigga, shawdy. You gotta stay loyal and fuck wit' that nigga, bruh."

"C'mo, man, you got ta know that. But I really just wanna tell ya I 'preciate ya for lettin' me in the car on this lil move, bruh. I was fucked up."

Bully nodded. "Ain't shit, homie. I been tryin' to get my brutha to ride wit' me for the longest, but you know that nigga, shawdy stuck on that pimpin' shit. Plus I know yo' ass be wit' this type shit. And I figured you might be fucked up after just gettin' out and shit."

"Boi, hell yeah, boi. I ain't have a bean."

"It is what it is then. You wanna hit this shit?" he offered the blunt to Rico. "It's some midget but this shit still smokin'."

"Hell naw, I'm good, bruh," he said while pulling out his pack of cigarettes. "I ain't doin' shit but smokin' cigarettes from now on. But look though, I need some straps, my nigga. You know where I can get some at?" He touched the tip of his Newport to the cherry of Bully's blunt and took a deep pull.

"Shiiit, I got a couple pistols I can get off."

Rico shook his head while exhaling a stream of smoke. "I don't need no pistols. I need some big shit like some choppas and AR's and shit."

Bully sat quietly for a second as the wheels of his mind churned. "You know what, bruh." He hit the blunt and pointed at Rico. "I think I heard some shit 'bout that boi Lorenzo hittin' a train for some carbon fifteens and shit 'bout a week and a half ago," he croaked while holding his breath and the smoke in his lungs. "I can call that nigga and see what's up." He picked up his phone.

"Do that for me, bruh."

Bully nodded and made the call. A few minutes later, he hung up and told Rico that Lorenzo wanted them to slide by his spot in Tressletree whenever they got a chance. "You want me to run ya over there now?" he asked.

"Now?" Rico asked and shot a quick glance at all the money and other shit on the table.

"Yeah, this shit ain't goin' nowhere, bruh, and I'ma stay over there wit' you."

Rico nodded. "Hell yeah, then, let's go see what that nigga talkin' 'bout." He stood up and grabbed a handful of money from the table. "I wanna get that nigga Monk a money order, too, shawdy. When I count this, we can just take this shit out of my cut."

"Nah, bruh, that's some real shit. I like that shit, bruh. Just go on 'head and get the money order and we still go split everything down the middle."

Rico nodded and put the money in his pocket as he followed Bully out of the house.

***

Leena walked into her bedroom and sat down on the couch next to Killa. "I put your t'ings and little money in dee closet."

"Lil? You know how much money that was?" he asked with a smirk.

"No," she said, preoccupied with turning the television.

"That was three hunnid and twenty somethin' thousand. That ain't no 'lil money'."

"Whatever, you just find somet'ing useful to do wit' it. Which, now dat I t'ink about it, I want to talk about somet'ing wit' you." She muted the TV and turned towards him as he tried his best to hide the fact that his feelings were kind of hurt by her just chumping off his *little money*. She looked into his handsome face and couldn't help smiling. "Okay, since me and you are, you know, back or whateva, and you're done wit' what's her face, right?" Killa nodded slowly. "Good. So, I was t'inking, you know, I got more den enough money for me, you, and a family to be straight for good. Soooo, what do you t'ink about quitting?"

"I'm sorry," he said as he closed his eyes and shook his head once quickly, thinking that he'd missed something. "Quittin' what?"

"You know what I'm talking about, Brenton, don't play dumb wit' me," she said seriously.

Correctly assuming that she was talking about him hustling, he answered. "A'ight, you asked me what I think about quittin', so I'ma tell ya. I don't like it, and this why. You got enough money. Regardless if it's for us or not, it's yours. If shit don't work out wit' us, what I'ma do? Tiara and my kids go forever be my responsibility, shawdy, not yours. I can't be dependin' on you to take care of my kids and treat 'em the way I wanna treat 'em, the way I wanna spoil they ass. You ain't obligated to them like I am. So, no, I don't like that shit you talkin' 'bout."

Leena nodded. "Okay, I listened to you, now listen to me. I love you. I love Tyga and little Beans like dey mine because dey yours. I'm obligated to dem just as much as you and Tiara because I love you. I don't care dat I didn't birt' dem, dey yours derefore dey mine, too. So dis shit you talking about, 'what you go do if we don't work out' and all dat udda shit, I'm telling you now, you don't need no safety net wit' me, Brenton. We go work, I promise. Now dat I got you back, I would die and go to hell just to make sure I don't eva lose you again."

"That shit sound good but..."

"I tell you what, I'ma show you just how serious I am. Tomorra, me and you gonna go see Brewster and I'ma set up a trust for you, Tyga, and Beans. I'ma add Tyga and Beans to my will and..."

Killa cut her off. "Hold up, you ain't gotta do all that shit. We straight just how we is. You got yo' money and I'm gettin' mine. We don't need to change nothin'. If shit ain't broke, we don't need to fix it."

"Yes, we do, Brenton," she pleaded, her eyes sparkling with moistness. "It took for me to almost lose my life to realize dat it's only one t'ing on dis eart' wort' dying for and dat's you. Now to turn around and have some shit happen to you and fuck around and be in dee position you was in when I was fucked up, all because you wanna go out dere and be in dee streets chasing dem fuckin' peanuts." She shook her head. "Listen, I can't see dat. Ain't no amount of money wort' losing you, and you shouldn't be concerned wit' money anyway. I got us. You can't do not'ing out dere in dee streets to alter our financial stability one way or anudda, no matta how hard you tried. I don't care what you did. I sold cocaine for years, Brenton, tons of dat shit, and all dat money I made, all dat money we got, none of it can buy me anyt'ing to give me dee feeling I get from your love. All I want you to do is t'ink about finding a new route. You're an intelligent, young black man, baby, I know you wasn't planning on selling dope your whole life. I want you to sit down one day soon and just t'ink about what I'm saying. I know you got some business plans or ideas or somet'ing, let's start trying to cultivate dem and make dem a reality."

Killa chewed at his bottom lip as he mulled over his most recent reality check. "You right," he mumbled as he started to nod slowly.

Leena smiled. "Promise me to at least t'ink about it?"

"I promise, bae," he said and pulled her closer. "Now, can I have a kiss?"

"You may." She giggled and climbed in his lap. She placed a kiss on the tip of his nose before his lips found hers, but a few seconds later she was pulling away from the passionate kiss they were sharing as his hands started to fumble with the button of her pants. "Uh-uhnn, you still ain't gettin' none of dis yet," she said, standing up.

"C'mo, bae, what you mean? You was just talkin' 'bout trust accounts and wills and how much you love me and shit, but now I can't even get none of the coota?"

"You damn right, nigga, not afta what your ass did, getting dat bitch pregnant, 'bout to marry her and shit." She closed her eyes and shook her head, still angry about it. "You got to show me dat not only do you want it, but dat you sorry for fucking wit' dat hooka again. You know I hate her, you s'posed to found somebody new to fuck wit'. You know I would've rolled ova in my grave if I had've died and you married dat girl, Brenton? So just for the scare you gave me," she walked over to her bed and picked up a pillow. "Your ass sleeping on dee couch." She tossed him the pillow and slid out of her stretchy jeans, showing off a pair of royal blue boy shorts.

Killa frowned. "You serious, man?" he asked unbelievingly.

Leena gave one hard, loud laugh. "As a heart attack, baby," she said while sliding onto her bed and under the covers.

"I ain't got time for this shit," he mumbled to himself while shaking his head.

"Say what, nigga?" she asked.

"Nothin', shawdy."

"Dat's what I t'ought," she said with a smug little grin on her beautiful face.

***

"Hell yeah, bruh, this exactly the type of shit I needed," Rico said as he inspected the AK-47 he'd bought from Lorenzo. A lit Newport was in his mouth and his head was tilted slightly to the side so the smoke wouldn't rise and burn his eyes. He cocked the unloaded weapon and squeezed the trigger. Click! He loved that sound.

"What you need all these straps fa, bruh?" Bully asked as he worked his phone trying to get rid of his share of the lean they'd taken.

"You know them fuck niggas over there in Fourf Ward kilt my brutha an lil susta, right. I gotta deal wit' them niggas. I can't let no shit like that ride."

Bully nodded his agreement. "Hell yeah. Who them niggas is?"

"Lil young nigga over there named Bam."

"I know bruh," Bully interrupted Rico. "Well, I don't really know him, but I know who he is. He s'posed to be somethin' like a lil shoota for that nigga Killa. Shawdy gettin' that paypa over there."

"He one of them niggas, too. He got the dreads, right?"

Bully stifled a yawn. "Yeah, Killa do. Bam be rockin' the temp wit' the waves. One of them niggas other pahtnas that used to get money just got kilt not too long ago, nigga named Chop. I used to get my work from homes when Juan ain't have shit."

"Yeah, that's them niggas. I'ma kill them niggas, bruh," Rico said quietly, shaking his head sadly. "Them niggas kilt my fuckin' susta, and Nico bitch ass."

They both sat quietly for a few seconds before Bully broke the silence. "Niggas used to talk that shit, man, but I miss that nigga Nico, bruh, wit' his ol' cappin' ass."

Rico laughed sadly. "I miss that nigga, too, shawdy."

Silence fell again before Bully's phone alerted him. "Ohhh," he said, looking at his phone. "I got a play on this lean. I'm 'bout to run over here to Cleveland. One of my lil Rollak pahtnas want this shit. You go stay over here or you got somewhere else to go, bruh?"

Rico stood up and yawned. "Take me over there to Zarianna house, man. I know she done heard by now I'm out. My baby prob'ly worried sick 'cause she ain't seen or heard from me yet."

Bully nodded. "Check that."

"I wanna leave all my shit over here, though."

"That's cool, all of it go be here whenever you get ready to get it."

"'Preciate it, bruh," Rico said and headed outside to the Grand Prix.

Chapter Thirteen

It had been a week since Killa had left Tiara and, aside from dropping by at times when he was sure Doonie would be home, he hadn't said a grand total of twenty words to her. He had been effectively using his son as an unknowing argument deterrent by keeping him close by while packing his things. Every time Tiara tried to talk to him, he would strike up a new conversation with his son and carry it on until she got so frustrated and angry that she just shut the hell up.

This particular Saturday afternoon was no different. Doonie sat on the bed, watching his father pack as they talked about his new favorite thing to do, play basketball. Killa, who had been a pretty good point guard in his younger days, was excited as hell to hear that his boy had taken a liking to the sport and they both were so deep in conversation that neither of them payed much attention to the house phone ringing.

"Doon, telephone," Tiara yelled.

"Who is it, ma?" he called back.

"This lil girl," she said in an exasperated tone.

"What lil girl?" Killa asked, but Doonie blushed and ran out of the room. "Damn, I ain't been gone but a few days," he whispered to himself as he walked back into the closet. A couple of seconds later, he heard the bedroom door close. "You must have told her you was go call her back? What's her name and she bet' not be ugly or I'ma change ya last name." When Doonie didn't answer, he stepped out of the closet and saw Tiara sitting on the bed, looking as pretty as ever in a pair of his Ralph Lauren sweats and one of his grey wife beaters.

"Please, baby, all I want, all I need is like two minutes." When Killa didn't respond or make a move to leave, she began to speak her mind. "Baby, listen, I'm sorry, for everything. I did some shit I shouldn't have. I been lyin', and I'm sorry for it all.

But please, please just listen and try to understand what I'm sayin'." Tears sprang to her eyes as she continued. "Baby, you make me so, so happy and I love you soooo much. You ain't even got no idea what it's like. All I ever wanted was for you to love only me, and be happy wit' it. I ain't perfect, baby, and I make mistakes, but that's all they is, is mistakes. Brenton, baby, this me. You know I know you like the back of my hand. I know you'a go ballistic in a split second, so everything I did and all the lies I told to cover it up, I did it just to keep you from gettin' mad, just to keep you happy like I love to see you, baby. I know I should not have done that shit, but just being honest, I didn't think you was go find out about it. But now you have, so I gotta tell you what happened." She broke down then, just the thought of what she was about to reveal made her cringe. She dropped her head to her hands and sobbed like a little girl.

Killa looked on as his beautiful black woman cried her heart out. He loved her, deeply. "Tiara, look at me, baby." She raised her head and looked at him through wet, puffy eyes. He sighed and threw a few of his dreads out of his face. "We been fuckin' 'round off and on for what, twelve, thirteen years, since I was fifteen. We got two beautiful kids and I love you so fuckin' much that it hurt, shawdy. But I just can't keep doin' this shit, man. I'm ti'ed. The lies, the games, I can't even trust you, T. You broke my heart, babe." A single tear slipped from the corner of one of his eyes, not only because he knew that he was hurting Tiara, but also because this breakup, this time, felt different somehow. He felt none of the typical anger or frustration that was usually associated with breaking up with her. He was calm and cool, very much in control. But for some reason, he had the eerie feeling that this was it, that they were finished for good this time.

"I'm sorry, baby, but you can learn to trust me again. Just come home, Brenton, and we can work this out. We always do," she sobbed quietly.

Killa shook his head slowly and wiped his eyes with the palms of his hands as more tears began to fall. "Not this time, Teet. Not this time." He squeezed the words past the basketball in his throat as he walked over to her. He brushed her hair back and held her face with both of his hands.

"What you mean not this time? What is you sayin'?" Tiara whispered. She had a panicked look on her face.

Ignoring the question, Killa placed a soft, tender kiss on her forehead. "I love you, Tiara," he whispered and slowly backed away.

"I love you, too, Brenton, baby. Wait, wait, baby, don't leave. Please don't leave yet. Tell me what you talkin' 'bout?" she begged in a hoarse whisper.

Killa had the feeling that she was feeling the same strange sense of finality that he was. He couldn't even look her in the face anymore for fear of seeing the tremendous amount of pain and hurt he was causing to one of the most precious women he'd ever had in his life.

He bent to scoop up his bag just as Doonie burst back into the room unannounced. The two adults played everything off smoothly. Tiara complained of allergies as she wiped her eyes and Killa spun around so his son couldn't see his face. "I'm gone, later on, Doon," he called over his shoulder as he walked out.

"Bye, daddy," Doonie said sadly.

Outside, Killa climbed behind the wheel of his Benz and a sense of complete calm engulfed him. It seemed as if the weight of the world had been removed from his shoulders. He sat in the peace and quiet of his car and enjoyed it for a few minutes. Right then, for the first time since meeting Tiara all those years ago, he could honestly say that he felt truly free of the vise grip she'd held him in for so long. No longer did he feel the sense of obligation to her. He was free to completely move on, and even though his new freedom had come at a steep price, he was going to enjoy every minute of it from then on.

His phone ringing interrupted his thoughts, and he smiled when he saw Leena's picture on the display. "Hey, love," he answered happily while cranking up the Mercedes.

"Hey, baby." Her smile could be heard in her voice. "Where are you?"

"Headed to our spot as we speak," he said, backing out of his old driveway.

"Dee girl almost done wit' my hair so why don't you just come back to the salon to get me first?" she suggested.

"Shiiit, that's cool. I'll be there in 'bout thirdy."

"Great. Can you bring me somet'ing to eat, baby? I want some Subway. I'm hungry."

"A'ight. I'll be there in a few."

"Okay, boo, love ya."

Killa smiled again before responding. "Love you, too, bae. Later," he said and hung up, tapping the gas a little harder.

***

"Maaannn, this the third time this mufucka done rode by today, and they been creepin'," Bam said when he saw the black Grand Prix turn onto Linden Avenue again.

His statement made the small group of six focus on the car. "Prob'ly ain't nobody but the folks takin' pictures again. Fuck 'em," one of the hustlers said while exhaling a stream of smoke from one of the blunts of gas that was in rotation and shooting a bird at the Pontiac and whoever was in it.

Bam scowled and shook his head. Something wasn't right. "That ain't no fuckin' police, twelve wouldn't keep ridin' up and down the street like that."

"Don't start trippin', boo. It ain't that serious. Huh, hit the weed and be cool," Sherrelle said and passed the blunt to him. She waved and blew a kiss at the slow passing car.

Bam hit the gas once and then lost it. "Man, fuck this shit. Y'all niggas watch out," he said with the blunt in his mouth as he pulled a ten shot .40 cal. from his pocket. "That ain't twelve, shawdy." Boc. Boc. Boc. Boc. Boc. Boc. Boc. Boc.

After the first bullet slammed into the Grand Prix, its driver smashed the gas and started to swerve erratically to try to avoid the rest of the bullets. It made a right onto Parkway and was quickly out of sight.

"What the fuck is you doin', crazy?" Sherrelle yelled as she and the other niggas got up from the ground, a couple of them coming out from behind a huge green dumpster. They all had been expecting return fire.

"Go 'head on, Relle. That wasn' the police," Bam warned in a no nonsense tone as he made his way towards his apartment.

"How the fuck you know, lil nigga? Them bitches might be on the way back now," she yelled at him again.

"That wasn' the fuckin' police, man. Trust me, man, I just know."

"You sound retarded, nigga," Sherrelle said while shaking her head. "I'm 'bout ta go. Stupid ass shit," she muttered under her breath and started to walk quickly down towards Central Park Place.

Everybody else followed her lead and left, and pretty soon, only Bam and Loose were standing in front of his porch. "They scary as fuck. That wasn' twelve, or they would'a shot back. Nigga don't even hear no sirens, man. C'mo, bruh, le's go on in. I need some mo' bullets just in case whoever the fuck that was come back."

***

"Mama, where we goin'?" Doonie asked from the backseat of his mother's Mercedes.

"I don't know, honey, ya daddy takin' us somewhere," Tiara said, preoccupied with driving.

"Oh." He was no longer interested in where they were headed. His stomach rumbled. "I'm hungry, ma, le's go to Burger King."

"We can't stop right now, baby, or ya daddy might leave us," she responded while abruptly changing lanes to keep Killa in sight.

"Just call daddy and tell him to wait for us," Doonie persisted.

Tiara shook her head. Maybe, if he knew they were following him, like Doonie thought. "Look in the baby bag on the side, Doon, it's some gummi bears in there. Just eat them 'til we can stop for real food, okay?"

Doonie shrugged and reached for the bag just as Tiara cut somebody else off. While he smacked away on the candy, little Bianca began to stir. "You want me to give her some, ma?"

Tiara thought for a second. "Yeah. Bite off some real small pieces and give them to her." About fifteen minutes or so later, Tiara watched Killa get out of his car with the Subway sack and soda he'd bought earlier, and walk into a salon called Hair Illusions in Southwest Atlanta. She had parked where she could see the entrance of the salon, and as she waited to see what would happen, all kinds of thoughts and questions shot through her mind. *Why the fuck is he here? And who is he here to see? What if, nah, it bet not be another bitch.*

"Mama, what we doin'?"

"Be quiet, Brenton Junior," Tiara snapped.

Doonie shut his mouth in a hurry. He'd learned the hard way that whenever his mother called his real name, she wasn't fucking around. And since he wasn't quite in the mood for an ass whipping, he sat back.

Tiara closed her eyes and prayed silently. *Please, god, don't let this fool be in there wit' some random ass bitch 'cause I'm goin' to jail today when I kill her ass.*

"Mama. I thought you said Leena was dead. She ain't no dead. There she go right there wit' daddy," Doonie said excitedly.

Tiara's eyes sprang open, and just as sure as fish could swim, she was looking at the walking dead. Leena was holding the Subway bag and her other arm was around Killa's waist as she laughed at something he'd said. Tiara's temper skyrocketed. A vein in her neck threatened to burst under the pressure as she thought about running them both over with her car. But instead, she bolted out of the driver's seat and ran towards the unsuspecting pair. "I should'a fuckin' known. I liked you better when you was a fuckin' vegetable, bitch. But don't worry, I'm 'bout to drag yo' lil red ass all over this fuckin' parkin' lot," she yelled.

Leena froze when she heard and saw Tiara running towards her and Killa in a full sprint. That was the first time she'd seen her since awakening from the coma, and even though she still hated her, she'd honestly outgrown all of the childish bullshit. She stood rooted to the spot in front of the salon with a wary expression fixed on her face.

"What the fuck, Tiara? I know good and got-damn well yo' ol' stupid, country ass ain't followed me all the way out here. Bitch, where the fuck my damn kids at?" Killa exploded.

Tiara either ignored him or was so caught up in her own rage that she didn't hear him. Either way, she didn't respond to him. "Ain't no sense in lookin' all stupid and shit now, bitch. I'm 'bout to whup that ass," she said as she got close enough to take a swipe at Leena.

"Watch the fuck out, man. What the fuck you doin' here?" Killa demanded as he stepped in front of Leena, the blow bouncing off of his chest.

"Nigga, move out my fuckin' way. Yo' ol' dirty ass, you ain't shit. When the fuck you was go tell me she was out the hospital, Killa? Done left me and yo' damn kids to go lay up wit' this ol' stankin' ass, mangy ass bitch. Moooove. Move out my fuckin' way," Tiara shouted and swung at Leena again.

That blow struck Killa's neck. "Watch out, girl," he growled through clenched and bared teeth.

"Get out my way, nigga. Mooove," she shouted and swung again, but that time Killa weaved and grabbed her.

"Stop actin' fuckin' stupid out here, Tiara. You see all these fuckin' people out here? They go call the police on yo' stupid ass if you don't stop," he shouted in her ear.

"I don't giva-fuck, nigga. Let me the fuck go right the muthafuck now, nigga, you fuckin' muthafucka!" When Killa's grip on her tightened, she knew she had no chance of getting out of his arms, so she screamed loudly.

"Leena. Leena," he had to yell to be heard over Tiara's screaming. "Go get in the car, shawdy. I'ma be there in a minute." Leena nodded and took the keys from him before hurrying to his car.

Tiara started to laugh loudly. "Go on and run, bitch. It don't matta. I'ma personally make sure yo' ass die this time. I promise ya that, ho. I'ma Google yo' stankin' ass and you go die this time, stankin' bitch," she yelled to Leena's retreating back. "Let me go, nigga."

"What's wrong wit' you?" Killa asked with a disgusted look on his face.

"Fuck you, nigga. I can't fuckin' believe you." She started to cry. Killa let her go and she began to shake her head. "You go throw away all this that we done built, ya family and everything, for that ol' homewreckin' ass bitch, Brenton?"

Killa shook his head. "It's over wit', T. Let it go. Stay the fuck from 'round me and Leena. If you fuck wit' her, I promise yo' ass I'ma personally fuck yo' life up. And if I catch you followin' me again, I'ma beat yo' fuckin' brains out yo' head. Leave us alone, man. I'm tellin' ya," he warned icily.

"Fuck you, nigga. I'ma get that bitch. I don't giva-fuck what you do to me," she whispered through her tears, a crazy looking smile on her face.

Killa nodded. "A'ight, play wit' it," he warned before turning and heading towards his car.

Ambitious

Chapter Fourteen

Killa and Leena stepped out into the warm night onto Peachtree Street and she was pleasantly surprised to see the shiny black carriage drawn by two beautiful white mares with black splotches all over their bodies.

Glancing between Killa and the carriage, Leena had a gigantic smile on her face as she whispered to herself, "Oh my god."

The driver of the carriage, a tuxedoed and top hatted white man, climbed out of the driver's seat and made his way around the carriage. "Good evening, Madam." He removed his top hat and gave a sweeping bow in front of Leena. "Sir," he stood and said, replacing his hat and touching its brim as he nodded slightly at Killa.

Giddy with excitement at the romantic gesture, Leena closed her eyes and buried her face into Killa's chest. "Aww, baby," she mumbled.

"C'mo, bae," he said with a smile and nodded for the driver to open the little door to the blood red, velvet interiored carriage.

Allowing Killa to help her up into the carriage, Leena looked around and saw all of the excited looks and happy faces staring at her and Killa and she felt special. She literally didn't stop smiling for the next hour and a half as they were chauffeured around Atlanta's safer and more scenic areas. She had a hard time not kissing or hugging or simply just touching some part of him every five minutes or so. He'd done nothing spectacular, but with her, as it had always been, it didn't have to be anything breathtaking from him. Just this simple, romantic act, and in the eyes of the public, had blown her mind.

They talked about everything from what had happened earlier that day with Tiara, which he apologized at least fifty times for, to, and much to her delight, a business venture he had been trying to map out. It was nothing major, just a simple sports bar and grill, but it was more than enough for her. It was the beginning of a step in the right direction and she was so proud of him just for even considering it. She was kind of sad when their little ride through the city was over, though. She honestly had wanted that moment to last forever, but as she already knew, all good things eventually had to come to an end.

Later that night, she sat up in bed watching Killa prepare *his couch* for bed and giggled silently. He had been such a good sport and gentleman the entire time, respecting her wishes to the point that sometimes she'd wished that he would just say fuck it and come take the pussy from her. Feeling a smidget of pity for him, she giggled again, but that time it got his attention.

He glanced over at her while fluffing his pillow. "What?" he asked with a half-smile on his handsome face.

She smiled, her green eyes twinkling as she shook her head. "Not'ing. Come over here, baby." She waved him over and, try as she might, she just couldn't help noticing how his black boxer-briefs molded to his body, accenting his powerful thigh muscles, or how his black wife beater hugged his muscled torso. And the tattoos, she shook her head quickly to gain control of herself and made a mental note to start going down to the complex gym with him every time he went from now on.

"What up bae?" He sat on the bed and said with a smile before pecking her on the lips.

Speechless, or better yet, just not knowing exactly how to say what she wanted to say, she stared into his smiling face, wrapped her arms around his neck, and kissed him again, slipping her tongue into his mouth as her passion quickly grew to a fever pitch. With his breaths coming in short, rapid bursts, Killa started to dominate her tiny frame, and she moaned with pleasure from the way he roughly but lovingly manhandled her. Damn, she missed this feeling. She wanted him so bad, and from the feel of things as her arm brushed against his crotch, he wanted her, too. She let him lay her back and pin her arms above her head as he attacked her neck and throat with hot kisses and soft tongue. Closing her eyes and giving in to him, she let him do his do while she enjoyed every millisecond of it.

Lifting up so he could remove her little peach colored thong, her hormones were raging as she rubbed his shoulders and chest. He made his way down between her legs, and the instant he tongued her, she screamed out in pleasure and sprayed a thin stream of her juices in his face. Caught completely off guard, Killa sputtered and spit before realizing what had had just happened. He looked up at her with smoldering eyes and she dug both of her hands in his dreads before pulling his face back to her opening. That was the first time in ages that she'd experienced that feeling and she wanted to feel it again, right then, instead of later. Unbelievably turned on, Killa devoured her organ and, to his utter delight, every time she screamed out, "I'm coming," she sprayed him with her fluids.

Well worn out but still craving more, Leena pushed him away and moved to straddle his face backwards. With her body positioned just right atop his, she began to scoot back and forth while rubbing and gripping at his muscled stomach and chest. When she felt his tongue at her asshole, she almost jumped through the ceiling. But the little pleasure seeker inside of her would have none of it. She moaned loudly as he rimmed her, and when she absolutely, positively could stand it no longer, she scooted backwards with a loud scream of ecstasy, placing her pussy back at his mouth. Leaning forward, she pushed his boxer-briefs down just enough to expose his dick and balls. She was going to need both of those as horny as she was.

Pre-come glistened on the head of his dick, and even more of the sticky substance was seeping from the tip of it now that it had room to come out. Leena grabbed it and stroked it a few times, causing more of the fluid to come out before taking him into her mouth. She sucked on him hungrily as he alternated between licking her pussy and ass, giving each one a generous amount of attention. On the verge of coming in his face again, she tried to raise up but she heard Killa grunt, "Uh-uhn," as he palmed her ass cheeks and pinned her to his face.

Straining against him to get away from his oral assault on her, and with his dick still in her mouth, she looked between both of their bodies and saw his tongue working quickly. She spit his dick out and screamed, "Ahhhhhh shiiiiiiiiit," as she released spray after spray of her come in his face. After her squirting dwindled down to a trickle, she collapsed onto him, heaving and out of breath.

Killa maneuvered out from under her hundred and thirty or so pound frame and told her, "Le's go," in a no bullshit tone. He was focused. She took her time getting to her hands and knees and paid for it when he slapped her on the ass hard enough to make it sting. She screamed out and jumped, but he was already massaging it when she looked back over her shoulder. He licked and kissed the handprint he'd left on her ass before standing back up, stroking his dick. Leena laughed a little, she kind of liked the stinging sensation.

"I been layin' on hittin' this ol' red ass again, ma," he said as he flicked both of his wrists, slapping both of her ass cheeks lightly, making them jiggle a little. "And you done got ya weight back," he mumbled to himself as he squeezed into her from behind. The pussy felt like an oven and gripped his dick like a gorilla fist as she went crazy every time he dug in it.

He was a man possessed, on her ass like white on rice. The more she tried to run, the more he pounded and followed right behind her. They had started out on the bed but wound up on the floor somehow, without missing a beat. Leena was standing straight up, gripping her ankles and looking up between her legs at his dick slamming into her. His balls slapped against her, making a squishy clapping sound and splattering her wetness everywhere as she screamed with pleasure. He accidentally slipped out of her, and the sensation of it pushed her over the edge. She screamed and creamed, sending a spray of come all over Killa and the carpet. But he himself was on the verge of a monster nut, so as her body locked up and she began to fall over, still clutching her ankles because, for some reason she couldn't move at the moment, he grabbed either side of her waist and slid back into her. Not many strokes later, he busted inside of her and his knees buckled. Refusing to fall, he just leaned backwards, sure to keep a hold on her waist as she still hadn't budged, and plopped back onto the soft, comfortable bed, beyond exhausted.

***

Everything had returned back to normal hours ago. It was a hot Saturday night and the block was beating. Bam, Loose, Reek, and some other hustlers from the hood were sitting on the low brick wall in front of his spot kicking the shit with a couple broads Loose knew from Kirkwood. Cat-Eyes was drunk as hell and geeked up on something, acting a damn fool. Every other minute or so somebody was having to tell him to chill out because he was kicking some unnecessary ra-ra shit and kept fumbling and bumbling with his pistol, scaring the new pussy.

Bam was on the verge of cursing his ass out, and he'd already made up his mind that he was gonna blow on his ass the next time he did some shit to scare one of the hoes into saying that they were ready to go. He looked at his pahtna and sighed while shaking his head.

"What's wrong wit' you cutie?" the chick named Re-Re that had immediately chosen him the second she saw him, asked.

Bam sucked his teeth and nodded towards Cat-Eyes. "This nigga here trippin' wit' this ol' junkie ass shit," he mumbled.

Re-Re's eyes got big and she grinned shyly. "I know right," she whispered. "I'm really kinda scared of his ass. Whatever he on, he don't never need to do that shit no mo'." Bam just shook his head. "Who these people is on yo' shirt?" she asked and pointed at his chest.

Bam looked down and straightened out his shirt. "This my pahtna, Tuna." He pointed at the picture on the left side of his chest. He pointed at the pictures in the middle and on the right side of the shirt and said, "And these my other pahtnas, Chop and Mario. God bless the dead."

"Damn, what happened, they got kilt?" Bam nodded *yeah*. "At the same time?" she asked incredulously with a shocked expression on her face.

"Hell naw."

"I was 'bout to say, damn, that's fucked up."

Bam chuckled a little. Something about Re-Re's personality was having a winning effect on him. She was a short pudgy little something but, so far, she seemed as sweet as sugar, and she was as cute as a button. A lot of the niggas he rocked with kicked the siddity role with fat chicks. He was even guilty of such, on occassion, but not this time. Re-Re seemed to be good folks, and from the looks of it, she took damn good care of herself. "You wanna go in the house and chill?" He nodded towards the apartment. "I got some mo' gas. Plus, we can get away from my ol' junkie ass pahtna." He pointed at Cat-Eyes again.

Re-Re smiled and dropped her head. "Nah, I'm good. I'm high as hell already, and I don't even smoke. I just smoked 'cause my home girls was smokin', but we can go in if you want to, though, as long as you just wanna kick it. I mean, I don't really know you so..." She left her sentence hanging, expecting for him to catch her drift.

"C'mo, man, do I really look like that type of nigga? I'm a perfect gentleman," he said with a smile. He liked her, and

140

especially so if she really meant what she'd just said. If she did, then he thought she might just be worth getting to know, but he was damn sure about to get her ass inside and put the press on her to try to find out.

She smiled again. "I don't know, we'll see. Nicki," she turned and called to one of her friends just before gunfire erupted.

Bam, and everybody else that had a shred of common sense, hit the deck first before reaching for straps or trying to figure out who the fuck was shooting. The only thing everybody knew for certain was that whoever was shooting was close. Clutching his .40, Bam dared to lift his head a little and take a look around, automatic gunfire still sang out and he was able to trace it back to its source, someone in a car, its brake lights aglow, a little ways up the street near Parkway. Flames danced dangerously from the barrel of some kind of choppa as its wielder stood beside the car, his door open and ready for him to dive in so he could make a quick getaway after wreaking havoc on the unsuspecting block.

Chambering a round, Bam began to squeeze off shot after shot at the nigga and the car and he saw his pahtna Cat-Eyes jump up and start running towards the mystery shooter, a hammer in each hand, letting rounds fly. Puzzled, Bam frowned. "What the fuck this stupid ass nigga doin'?" he whispered loudly to himself an instant before he watched Cat-Eyes drop to the ground abruptly and the nigga jump into the passenger seat of the car and speed off.

Sitting all the way up, discombobulated, and not quite understanding exactly what had just happened, Bam looked around. To his right lay Re-Re, her eyes, now cold and lifeless, were looking in his direction as a puddle of blood grew around her limp body. He groaned and dropped his head, not even needing to see his pahtna Cat-Eyes to know that he was dead as a fucking doorknob. His dumb ass had run on the nigga while he was bussing a stick like he was fucking Superman or some damn body.

He slowly started to shake his head and get up as he began to hear sirens in the distance.

***

Killa and Leena lay curled up together in their massive bed, enjoying the feel of each other and talking. She was idly twirling a few of his dreads around her finger and rubbing his chest as she listened closely to his business plans about the sports bar. He'd already admitted that he didn't know the first thing about running a business, but he was anxious and eager to learn all about it. Now that the seed had been planted, Leena could tell that he was growing more and more excited about the possibility of becoming a legitimate business owner, and she was right along with him. Regardless of how small it would be, it would be legit and one hundred times safer than getting money out of the streets, and that was really all that she cared about anyway, keeping him out of jail and out of the graveyard.

"So uhhh...when do you plan on making a move to get dis sports bar movement moving?" she asked.

"I guess as soon as I get enough money to buy me a good spot to put it. I need to start lookin' into this shit," he said through a yawn.

Leena sat up, her eyes sparkling with devilment. "Alright, we bot' know dat money ain't an issue but, since I know dat your stupid ass man pride won't allow you to take whatever you need from me, I'll loan you dee money to buy a location." Killa frowned and was just about to protest when she started talking again. "For one hundred and fifty percent back, and part ownership of dee business. Say, seventy-t'irty you," she shrugged. "And, of course, you would handle any and all executive decisions while I just sit back and offer advice and make suggestions. What do you t'ink?"

Killa frowned. "I don't know, man," he said slowly. "That hunnid and fifty shit."

"Is negotiable, not'ing else is."

He nodded slowly. "Sound a'ight, long as we do somethin' 'bout that one-fifdy shit."

"Good," Leena smiled. "We'll see Brewster tomorrow about it. Now in dee meantime, where are we wit' getting out of dee drug business? We seem to talk about everyt'ing except dat," she said, laying back down and throwing one of her legs over his. The moist warmness from her pussy against his thigh was enough to get rise out of him and start his hands wandering, but she grabbed his wrist, stopping him from starting something. "We can play later. I want you to answer my question."

Killa rubbed his jaw. "Shiiit, I'm workin' on that, too. You know I can't just go cold turkey. It's a lot of niggas dependin' on me. I'm makin' a way for a lot of the niggas I'm rockin' wit', but I'ma quit, eventually, especially wit' this sports bar shit on my mind."

Leena looked at him skeptically and started to say something but his phone rang and stopped her. She glanced at the clock, 2:12 a.m. it read, and wondered who was calling so late as he got up to go get it from over by the couch.

"What's up, lil bruh?" he answered after looking at the display. After listening quietly for a few seconds, he sat on the couch. "Damn, man," he whispered to himself. "What they start shootin' fa? Who the fuck it was?" he asked with a frown and listened quietly again as the caller explained all that he could. Leena watched him like a hawk. That was exactly the type of shit she was trying her damnedest to keep him away from.

"You a'ight, though, right? Everything straight wit' you?" he asked. "A'ight, man, I'ma be through there tomorrow and halla at y'all niggas, bruh. Y'all niggas be safe, shawdy," he said before disconnecting the call. Sighing loudly, he stood up with a shake of his head.

"What's wrong, baby?" Leena asked.

"One of my lil pahtnas just got kilt, man," he answered as he walked back to the bed and laid down beside her.

"Bam?" she asked in a fearful tone and with a scared expression on her face.

"Nah, that was Bam I was talkin' to. Cat-Eyes, I don't know if you knew him or not but you done seen him 'round. He the one got knocked off."

"Who did it?"

He shrugged. "I don't know. I don't wanna talk about it no mo'," he said quietly and curled up next to her.

"Okay, baby," she said sadly as she gently hugged his head to her bosom. *I'm here to save and protect you only if you would just damn let me, boy,* she thought to herself as she sighed deeply and held her man.

***

Nobody could even begin to dispute the fact that Bully was a real street nigga. He'd been running through them and getting money out of them in Atlanta for most of his life. He'd done a lot of crazy shit, and seen even crazier, but he just simply wasn't with the retarded ass shit Rico had just done. He was all for riding with him to get some straightening for his brother and sister, but damn, he had just opened fire on a whole crowd of people, and the majority of them, he knew, had nothing to do with what had happened to his family. He knew for a fact that Rico had shot at least three people, and it wasn't a doubt in his mind that he would've shot more had he not run out of bullets when he did.

A nigga gotta draw the line somewhere, he thought to himself as he hit his blinker and slowed to make the turn onto Bass Street off of Hill. Rico said that Zarianna was his gutta bitch and it was her driveway that Bully pulled into and parked his shot up Grand Prix. The bullet holes had come courtesy of the nigga Bam earlier that day when he and Rico had rode through Fourth Ward. That was actually another reason why he'd volunteered to ride with Rico, the psychopath, because Bam had shot his car up for no fucking reason.

Now, he was starting to think that maybe he should've just went on about his business after he and Rico hit the little lick over on Cascade, and let the lunatic deal with his own issues alone, although it still wasn't too late to do just that.

Rico jumped out of the Pontiac with his stick wrapped in a blanket in one hand and ducked his head back into the car. "'Preciate ya ridin' wit' me, bruh. Just halla at me and I'ma take care of ya back windshield and these bullet holes."

Bully waved it off. "Don't worry 'bout that shit, shawdy. You just be careful, bruh. Got all ya shit?"

Rico nodded. "Yeah, I got everything. 'Preciate it, my nigga. I'ma fuck wit' y'all," he said and closed the door. As Bully backed out of the driveway, Rico made his way to the front door, wondering how he'd forgotten about his ace in the hole. He'd seen somebody while he and Bully were over on Linden earlier, somebody he planned on using to gain the inside track on catching up with Bam and Killa. "I hope I ain't throw that nigga info away," he said to himself as he used the key Zarianna had given him to let himself into her house.

Ambitious

Chapter Fifteen

The next day, Killa was sitting on the couch at the trap spot having a serious talk with Bam. Loose, Reek, Rude-Boi, and a couple of other hustlers from the hood were in and out, keeping traffic through the place.

"Listen, bruh, we 'bout to be touchin' a whole lot mo' work. All that ol' dumb ass shit you be doin'," Killa started to shake his head. "You gotta stop that shit, shawdy. You can't keep losin' ya head, my nigga. That shit Sherrelle told me that happened yestaday'a be the same type of shit to get a nigga caught up. You remember what happened to Meech and them, nigga. Some bullshit made the whole empire crumble. You gotta start thinkin' before you do shit, my nigga. How the fuck you go be a boss?" He pointed at Bam's shirt, which had *I'ma Boss Not a Capo* emblazoned in large block letters across its front. "But you can't think and make good decisions when you angry or under pressure, cuz. C'mo, man." He slapped Bam's knee. "You gotta smarten up, young nigga."

Bam sat, rubbing his hands together, in deep thought. He cleared his throat. "You right, bruh. I need to tighten up, don't I, man?"

Killa hurried up and agreed with him. "Hell yeah, nigga, 'specially if you go be runnin' point over here for me. You gotta think like a boss to be a real boss, bruh."

Bam winced and nodded his head. "I know it, man. I'ma tighten up. I got ya, my nigga."

"Oh, shit. What's up, my nigga? When the fuck you got out?" Reek said excitedly into his phone as he walked into the apartment. Paying his two pahtnas sitting on the couch no mind, he headed to the back for something. Killa and Bam continued to talk and eventually their topic of discussion lightened. He was in the middle of telling Bam how cute something Bianca had done was when Reek walked back into the room.

"Aye, y'all know my lil pahtna Ricardo from Pittsburgh?" he interrupted them.

Killa was the first to answer after thinking about it. "I don't know no Ricardo from Pittsburgh. I know Ricardo that be gettin' a lil paypa over there on Sylvan Road. He a older nigga, though."

"Nah, I don't think I know him. I know Ricardo from Summa Hill. That nigga Rico name Ricardo," Bam said with a little glance at Killa.

Reek sucked his teeth. "Hell naw, not that nigga, my lil pahtna from Pittsburgh."

Bam shrugged with a pensive look on his face. "What he look like?" he asked.

"'Bout my height, brown skinned, got a missin' tooth."

"In the front at the bottom?" Bam asked.

"Yeah."

"Man, that's that nigga, bruh. That's Rico fool," Bam stood up and exclaimed with a crazed expression on his face.

"Man, no fuck it ain't. This my pahtna. He from the Burgh."

"Man, fuck all that. What about this nigga?" Killa asked anxiously as Bam pulled out his phone and started to fiddle with it.

Reek began to speak nervously, hoping that he hadn't fucked up. "I just told bruh it was cool for him to come through. He say he know both of y'all. He just got outta Rice Street 'bout three days ago."

Boc. Boc. Boc. Boc. Boc. Boc. Boc. Gunfire erupted.

Killa dove to the floor as projectile after projectile whizzed into the apartment. Boc. Boc. Boc. Boc. Boc. Boc. Boc. Glass shattered and all types of debris floated in the air. Boc. Boc. Boc. Boc. Boc. Boc. Boc.

Without raising an inch off of the floor, Killa began to scoot and slide towards the back of the apartment, away from the street side windows. He saw that Bam and Reek were both alive and well and also thinking along the same lines as himself as they inched away from the street facing side of the apartment. Bam had a look of the utmost fury on his face and Reek, poor ol' Reek, was crying.

After what seemed to be a few minutes, but was actually only a few seconds, Killa began to hear little bursts of handgun fire mixing in with the unmistakable sound of the assault rifle. Not long after that, tires screeched loudly, and then deadly silence dominated.

Panting, Killa just closed his eyes and rested his forehead on the hard floor. "Damn," he exploded.

***

On Chappell Road, Leena tapped on the brakes, slowing her AMG to a stop to allow the champagne colored Buick to pull out of Chappell Forest apartments. The guy driving the Buick tooted his horn and held his hand up out of the already rolled down window to say thanks as he eased out in front of her.

Making eye contact with each other for a split second, Leena froze with a sharp intake of breath. "But Killa said," she said to herself as tears welled in her eyes, blurring her view of the rear of the Buick as it made its way down towards Bankhead. It couldn't be. Her heart pounded as every part of her body shut down and her mind trudged back to the horrible night that she'd been attacked in her home. Reliving every single second of it, she felt every blow again, saw every movement, heard every word over, everything. She recalled how the intruder had beaten her until he'd gotten tired. How he'd pulled his mask off and mopped his sweaty brow with his T-shirt before pulling out his phone. How he'd made a call, and during that call he'd said, "Alright

Tiara." She mumbled the words as that particular strand of memory slammed into her for the first time since coming out of the coma.

Blaring horns from the cars behind her ripped Leena from her memories back to the present day and time. Blinking back tears, she cut the wheels of the Mercedes hard to the left and smashed the gas, making a U-turn right in the middle of Chappell Road, and flushed back towards Martin Luther King Jr. Drive. Killa needed to know this immediately.

***

The police had come through and done a report because somebody who'd heard the gunfire called and reported it, probably one of the old people around the hood, so nobody payed it any mind. Nobody had been killed or even injured that time, but the police had lingered a little longer than usual, being that it was the second time in less than twenty-four hours that they'd had to rush over to Linden Avenue because gunshots had been reported.

Now Killa and a bunch of other hustlers from the hood were staring at the screens of their gadgets, Rico's face and case on some of them, and Monk's on others.

"That's him, bruh," Reek was saying as he shook his head slowly, looking over Killa's shoulder at the tablet in his hands. "I swear to god, bruh, when we was in Rice Street, the whole dorm was callin' that nigga Pittsburgh. Niggas I know for a fact from over that way was callin' shawdy that shit, bruh."

"Well you can stop sayin' that shit 'cause this nigga ain't from Pittsburgh, man. He had to be just sayin' that shit and usin' you to try to fish out shit 'bout us," Bam said.

"I'm just glad that nigga ain't got no fuckin' patience. he could'a waited a lil longer and tricked yo' ass into bringin' him face to face wit' us," Killa said, and Bam agreed. "But now that this bitch done got out, we can go and deal wit' his ass for real this time, and be through wit' this shit." The building fire could be heard in Killa's voice as he prepared his mind to deal with the last and final piece of a puzzle that he thought had already been put to bed. He jumped up. "I'll be back, bruh," he said, reaching in his pocket for his ringing phone. He tossed Bam's tablet on the sofa and answered. "What's up, bae?"

"Where are you?" Leena asked through sniffles.

"'Bout to head to the house now. What's wrong?" he asked, fearing that Rico might've gotten to her.

"I need to talk to you. It's important. You need to head home now. I'm already on dee way dere now."

Nodding quickly, Killa spoke, "A'ight, I'm leavin' now. You a'ight though?" he asked worriedly.

"I will be. Just meet me at dee house."

"Say no mo'," he said and hung up. "I think somethin' wrong wit' Leena, bruh. She want me to come home quick."

"Shiiit, I'm ridin' wit' ya," Bam said, standing up.

"Nah, just follow me, and if everything cool, you can just dip."

"That will work," he said, walking out behind Killa.

***

Leena was already home by the time Killa got there. He parked next to her Benz and hurried up to their loft. When he let himself in and saw that there was no immediate danger, he put his .38 back in his pocket and let Bam know that everything was cool.

He could tell that Leena had been crying, and she ran and hugged him fiercely when she realized that he'd crept into their home on her. Hugging her back, he smoothed her hair and kissed the top of her head, assuring her that everything was alright, and trying to get her to tell him what was going on.

After calming down a little, she led him into the living room and they sat on the couch together. She wasted no time with beating around the bush. "I saw dee dude dat tried to kill me."

"What? Where?" Killa asked, confused and anxious, his face turning into a mask of hardness.

She began to shake her head. "Dat's not important. What is, is dat when I saw him I had a flashback of dat night. I relived everyt'ing, every single moment of it. I remembered t'ings dat I previously hadn't. Dee most important of which is dat Tiara was involved wit' what happened to me."

"Hold up, man," Killa immediately said skeptically as he started to shake his head. "What the hell you talkin' 'bout?" he asked, thinking that it was some kind of plot of hers to even further pit him against Tiara.

"I swear I know what you might be t'inking but listen to me, dis ain't a game. When dat nigga was beating me, he stopped and took out his phone. He called Tiara and was talking to her. I know it was her because he said her name. When I saw his face again today, everyt'ing from dat night came roaring back to my memory, all dee little t'ings dat I had forgotten. I'm telling you, baby, I remember what happened and dat dude, whoeva he was, was in cahoots wit' Tiara."

Literally trying to wrap his mind around what Leena was saying, he blinked rapidly with a frown on his face. His brain honestly just flat out refusing to process and compute the information. If what Leena was saying was the truth, then that would mean that everything that had happened, her almost getting killed, all of the other killings and getting shot at, all because of Tiara. Get the fuck outta here. "Nah, man, I don't think..."

"Baby, I'm telling you. Dis ain't a game. I remember what dee fuck happened. What reason would I possibly have to make up a lie like dis? I already got what I want, Brenton, you here wit' me. Dee bitch had somet'ing to do wit it," Leena snapped but her eyes begged for Killa to believe her.

Not knowing what to do, he pulled out his phone and dialed Tiara's number. The phone rang a few times, and when she answered, he put it on speaker. "Hey, Brenton." She sounded down and out but relieved to hear from him. She rarely had at all lately.

"Listen, man, we need to talk. You at home?"

"Yeah, we here."

"Stay there, man. I'm on the way. It's important."

"Okay," she said.

Killa hung up. "Did that nigga see you?" he asked.

Leena nodded. "I t'ink so, but I don't t'ink he recognized me. He kept driving."

Even more reason for him to believe that Leena was just tripping. Everybody that he'd ever shot, never mind killed, he remembered. Their faces would forever be burned into his memory. Nodding, he thought for a second. "Where ya pistol at, bae?"

She ran off to get her small Glock and came back with it in her hand. Killa took it from her and ejected the clip. Making sure it was loaded, he popped the clip back in and chambered a round.

"When I leave, don't open the door. I don't giva fuck if Jesus Christ himself knock on that mufucka, don't open it. If somebody try to kick it down or break in, just point and shoot the shit out they ass. Then call the police. Don't open the door. Got it?"

"Yeah, yeah, I got it," she said nervously.

Killa handed her the pistol and then hugged her. "I love you. Don't open the door for nobody."

"I love you, too. I won't."

"Lock me out," he said and left, but only left the building after hearing Leena slide all three of the locks on the door into place.

***

He was above the speed limit all the way from Atlantic Station to Lithonia, and was pulling into his old driveway about thirty-five minutes after leaving his new place.

Tiara met him at the door and stepped back to let him in. "Hey," she said quietly, nervous as hell and wondering what he wanted to talk about so bad. She hoped he wanted to work things out.

She was looking beautiful, as usual, but that time Killa saw it but didn't see it. He hoped like hell she was innocent of what Leena was accusing her of for both of their sakes. "What's hap'nin?" he said, stepping into the townhouse. "Where Doonie at?" he asked, looking around as he headed to their old bedroom.

"In his room takin' a nap."

"Bumble Bee?"

"Her lil fat ass sleep, too. She in the nursery."

He looked in on his sleeping daughter and resisted the urge to go to her. He wasn't there for a social visit, it was strictly business. He led the way to their old bedroom and closed the door behind Tiara when she walked in behind him.

She sat on the bed, and when Killa grinned at her, she thought she knew what was so important. *Humph, this nigga want some pussy. Red bitch ain't doin' it like me, I guess*, she thought to herself as she felt a slight tingle between her thighs. *Well if he want it he can always get it*, she was thinking as she looked into his eyes.

He looked away and his smile vanished. "I don't really know how to say this shit, shawdy." He paused.

"Just say it, Brenton," Tiara said softly.

He sighed and dropped his head, closing his eyes and shaking his head, he spoke. "This shit might sound crazy, right, but Leena told me you had somethin' to do wit' her gettin' shot. She say the

154

nigga that did that shit to her pulled his phone out and called you. She say he said yo' name an everything." He lifted his head and looked at her.

Tiara's heart was in her throat and her stomach felt like it was in a blender. "That bitch tellin' a got-damn lie," she protested, but her eyes betrayed her. Killa saw the fear and uneasiness as clear as day in them.

"Tiara, listen, that shit over and done wit'. you ain't gotta be gettin' all loud and upset. I just wanna know the truth."

"She fuckin' lyin', Brenton. I don't know shit 'bout...'"

Killa snapped. "Got-damnit, Tiara," he exploded and punched a hole in the wall. Tiara screamed a little and quickly scooted across the bed, away from him. He had a crazy, deranged look in his eyes, but the next time he spoke, his voice let on to nothing of how he was feeling inside. "I'm sorry, bae. I ain't mean to scare ya," he said in a calm, apologetic tone. "It's just that I'm ti'ed of bein' lied to, T. You done broke my heart wit' enough lies already, shawdy. For once, man, just this one time, can you please just tell me the damn truth? Please, Tiara?" He finished with tears in his eyes.

Not knowing exactly what, but something possessed her to come clean. Maybe it was the tears streaming from Killa's eyes, or maybe it was the fact that she was plain old sick and tired of lying to and keeping secrets from the man she loved. Either way, she unloaded her burden. "Okay," she said in a hoarse whisper as she began to nod her head slowly. "I did. I was so mad when you told me that y'all was gettin' married, I had a nigga I know go and rob her."

Killa stared at her with a disbelieving horror struck look on his face for a second before it clouded over to fury. "You ol' twisted ass, evil ass bitch," he hissed as he crossed the room in the blink of an eye.

Tiara tried to get away from him, but there was nowhere to go. The first time he hit her she saw a flash of bright white light, the second time, blackness swallowed her. He wrapped his hands around her neck and started to squeeze. "Stupid, bitch, I fuckin' hate you," he screamed as tears ran wildly from his eyes. This was it, he'd had enough. Thinking of every single way that she had ever violated him, he squeezed, harder and tighter. She started to gag and gasp for air. Good. He was going to kill her. Great.

"Daddy, stop. What you doin' to mama? Stop, daddy. Stop," Doonie cried out as he tugged at Killa's waist.

It took for him to hear Doonie's whining to cut through the haze of the kill zone that he was in, and he released the pressure on Tiara's neck before stumbling backwards. When he felt the wall behind him, he slid down against it and watched as his son cried and called out to his mother. Once he saw what he needed to see, he quickly got up and left the house.

Chapter Sixteen

"Hey, bae, everything a'ight?" Killa asked as he floated through traffic on I-20 West.

"Yeah, everyt'ing's good. Where are you?" Leena's voice came through the speakers of the Benz.

"I'm on twenny, right," he said, glancing in his rearview before coasting over to a new lane. "I'ma swing by the hood and take care of some shit for a minute, then head home. You sure everything a'ight, ain't nothin' happened?"

"Yeah, not'ing's happened. Did you talk to her?"

Killa was quiet for a second. "Yeah, we'll talk about it when I get home. I'll be there in a lil while. Don't open..."

"Dee door. I know. I won't," she said.

"A'ight. I'll see ya in a bit. Love ya."

"Love you, too."

Killa disconnected the call and tapped the gas a little more. Getting on the connector, he caught I-75 North and headed to 4th Ward. Bam, Loose, Reek, Rude-Boi, Brandon, Sherrelle, and a bunch of other people were posted up outside the spot. Everybody, except Sherrelle, was strapped and, while the big guns weren't on display like the little pistols, they were extremely close by, some in bushes, some behind trashcans, and some more were in the apartment.

"What's up, bruh?" Bam said when Killa got out of the car. He was ready to get on the bullshit.

Feeling the vibe, Killa took a look at all the people and guns clustered around. "Aye, y'all niggas stand down, man. It ain't 'bout to be nothin'. Come halla at me, lil bruh," he said to Bam as he walked to the front door of the apartment.

"Aye, look, man, y'all niggas see anything crazy lookin', bus', fuck that shit. Take no chances, ask questions later, shawdy," Bam said.

Killa heard a chorus of agreement behind him as he stepped inside with Bam in tow. When the burglar barred screen door banged shut behind them, Killa sat on the couch and sighed. "Why the fuck you got all them people out there strapped up like that, bruh?"

A bit offended, Bam frowned. "What you mean, bruh. Them the same mufuckas was here before you left earlia. Some of them is the same mufuckas that started bussin' back at the nigga and made him run off."

"Yeah but they wasn't how they is now. Them folks ready to turn up out there."

"Shiiit, they s'posed to be, bruh. Yo' ass is, too." Bam continued to frown, Killa might as well had been speaking a foreign language because he damn sure didn't understand what the hell he was talking about. As far as he was concerned, it was time to start killing shit, end of discussion. "Fuck nigga done got out and already back on the bullshit...nigga done kilt Cat-Eyes, shot the spot up and shit, man. Le's go on and kill this fuck nigga, big bruh, before he wack one of us."

Killa shook his head slowly. "Nah, man."

"What you mean *naw*, man?"

"Bruh, just shut the hell up and listen for a minute, man, damn. You dead ass wrong anyway, young nigga. What, you 'bout to go kill some shit wit' twenty niggas wit' ya? We just fuckin' talked a few hours ago 'bout you usin' ya head, bruh. Think! How many of them niggas out there you think go be solid if y'all get caught and them folks go to talkin' them football numbas, fool? Somebody go fold, nigga, and I'm tellin' ya what I know. Last time we rode on them niggas, it wasn' but a few of us. That's all it take, shawdy, not no bunch of niggas. But we ain't 'bout to get caught up in this shit wit' this nigga again, and if yo' ass would just be the fuck quiet for a minute, I'ma tell ya why," he said when Bam looked like he was about to start talking shit. So instead, Bam sighed loudly and sat back against the couch.

"What we 'bout to do is get in touch wit' this nigga and wave the white flag. We go tell him he won and we don't want no smoke wit' him."

Bam looked at Killa like he was crazy. "What?" He sprang forward and exploded.

"Yeah, bruh, them niggas kilt Tuna, Mario, Cat-Eyes, and some mo' of our folks, but I know for a fact we kilt a whole slew of them niggas back. But this the thing, though, and you go flip the fuck out when I tell you this shit, bruh, I swear. But this whole time, this whole lil beef shit wit' them niggas been a big ass misunderstandin'," he said and began to tell Bam what he had just found out only a short while ago.

By the time he finished relaying the information, Bam's mind had officially been blown. "Woooooow," he said slowly. "Aye, look, man, I know that's baby mama, right, but that bitch need a killin', bruh, straight the fuck up. A nigga need to wack that bitch. That ho crazy, bruh." Killa just shook his head. "So what we need to be tryin' to do is find out who the fuck this other nigga she got to do that shit is."

"I know it, man. Once I seen that I hadn't kilt that ho, I just left, bruh. I had to leave before I wound up killin' that bitch. I don't trust myself to go back over there so I'll find out who that nigga is in a couple days. In the meantime, we need to track this nigga Rico down and at least try to get a lil understandin' wit' that fool 'cause it's time to eat. We don't need noooo bullishit fuckin' wit' this paypa."

Bam bit his bottom lip and nodded his agreement. Staring off into space, he winced suddenly. "Damn, bruh," he whined and started to shake his head slowly. "That bitch need to be kilt."

Killa shook his head again. "Boi, who you tellin'," he said as he got up from the couch and headed outside. Leena was at home alone, he needed to get to her.

***

"It's me, bae, open up," Killa said softly after Leena called out asking who it was at the door. He heard her unlocking it, and a second later, it swung it open. He was glad to see that she had the little Glock in her hand as he stepped inside, closing and locking the door behind him. They hugged quickly, Killa kissing her lips, and walked to the couch in the living room together.

"So, what she say?" Leena asked as she sat down and folded her legs underneath her.

Sighing, he grabbed the pistol she still clutched in her hand and began to nod slowly. "She did it," he said as a strong feeling of embarrassment and shame engulfed him. Everything that had happened to Leena now seemed like it was his fault, in a way, and he felt terrible just looking at her now.

Her mouth gaped open as she stared at him. She couldn't believe it now that she knew for sure. "What she say, Brenton?"

"She said she had some nigga she know do that shit 'cause she was mad about us bein' 'bout to get married. So I guess that's the nigga you seen earlia today. Listen, bae, I'm so fuckin' sorry that shit happened, man."

"Why you apologizing, baby?"

"'Cause, man, I feel like that shit was my fault. Tiara my baby mama, and her ol' stupid ass the one that did that shit, man," he said with a sad frown on his face.

"Dat's bullshit, Brenton. I don't blame you at all for what dat dumb bitch did. It ain't your fault in dee least. But I guess I am kind of upset wit' you a little," she said softly as she as she crawled over and sat in his lap.

"Why?" he asked as she laid her head against his chest.

"You really want me to tell you?" Killa nodded. "Well, dis is just how I feel, baby. You and your friends killed all dem people, some of your friends even got killed, too, and all of it was for no reason. I mean, y'all t'ought it was Nico, but it wasn't. But now, you know who it was and dat bitch just get a free pass, like she didn't have anyt'ing to do wit' any of it. I don't t'ink dat's right. That evil ass bitch dee reason so many people dead today, and it's like it's okay." Leena shook her head as tears welled in her eyes.

"Hell naw, that shit ain't okay, but how you know I ain't already dealt wit' her ass?"

Laughing sadly, Leena answered. "I ain't crazy, Brenton. I know you love dat evil ass bitch. But what I can't undastand for dee life of me at dis point is, afta what she did to me, to us," she took her head off of his chest and looked into his sad eyes, "our child, how can you still feel anyt'ing udda dan hate for her? I didn't do anyt'ing to her to deserve what she did to me, and knowing dat she gets a pass from you afta all of dee udda shit you did to dee wrong people, dat shit hurt baby." She laid her head back against his chest.

Killa sighed deeply, he understood all too well exactly where she was coming from, but he was stuck between a rock and a hard place. "What you want me to do, Leena, kill her?"

"Don't she deserve it, afta what she did? Afta all dee udda deat's she responsible for?" she sat up and said angrily.

"She do, but she the mutha of my kids, shawdy."

"I was too," she jumped up and screamed hysterically.

Killa shook his head slowly. "That's different, man," he said quietly before she cut him off.

"Ain't no fuckin' difference. To you, maybe it is because it's your precious fucking Tiara," she yelled and kicked over the coffee table in front of the couch. "But dee reality of it is it's not. I was pregnant wit' your child, minding my own fucking business, when dat bitch did what she did. If anybody else had been responsible, we already know what would've happened to dem. Dat bitch deserve to die. I know it. You know it." She jabbed her outstretched index finger at him. "I'm fucking tired of you treating dis bitch like fucking gold, like she can't do not'ing wrong. For some shit like what she did to me, she supposed to be able to get it just like anybody else got-damnit."

Blinking slowly, Killa stood up. "You right, bae, you absolutely right." He pulled Leena into an embrace and she wrapped her trembling body around his. "But another reality, as harsh as it may seem, is that I'm not 'bout to be responsible for takin' my kids mutha away from this earth. I want you to look in my eyes and believe me when I tell you that that's the only reason that bitch ain't already dead, Leena. Facts! As far as she concerned, my hands tied, but I'ma get that other nigga, whoever the fuck he was."

Leena wriggled out of his arms and backed away slowly. "You really don't get it, do you?" she said with new tears falling from her eyes. Shaking her head, she turned and headed for their bedroom. "I'm going to lay down. Alone. Don't come around me right now."

With a helpless look on his face, Killa shook his head and stared at her retreating back.

***

It had been two days since anything had popped off and, even though things had been quiet, the whole hood was still on high alert. The word had spread that Killa didn't want any bullshit going on, and nowadays, as far as his circle was concerned, which was a pretty big one, his word was something like law. The bricks had come and everybody was eating and, so far, everything was going good with Bam being at the helm of the ship. They hadn't been able to get a bead on Rico, and while they were actively trying to track him down, they would stay ready for whatever until they were able to do so and come to some type of understanding with the nigga.

Killa and Leena were beefing hard. For the past two days, the atmosphere inside of their all of a sudden too small loft was extremely tense and trying. They hadn't spoken a total of twenty words to each other, which wasn't due to a lack of trying on Killa's behalf, and they were even sleeping separately.

Early one afternoon as he got ready to leave the loft, he stopped by their bedroom door and looked in on her. He knew she'd seen him, but as usual as of late, she ignored him. Sighing as he leaned against the doorframe, he called out to her. "Bae?" She looked at him but didn't say anything. "Maaannn, what's up, man? I wish you would mufuckin' talk to me, shawdy. Say somethin', man."

She gave him her very best deadpan stare. He threw his hands in the air and walked into the bedroom. "Maaaan, what you want me to do, Leena?" he pleaded. "I can't kill the bitch."

"If dee shoe was on dee udda foot, would I get dee same treatment? No. But yet you claim to love me so fucking much."

Killa frowned. "How the fuck you go sit yo' ass up here and say some shit like that when the fact of the matter is, if you loved me and cared so much about me, we wouldn't even be havin' this discussion?"

Appalled, Leena bounced up from the bed. "I'm sorry. I was dee one dat was shot in dee fucking head. How in dee fuck did my feelings for you come into question here?" Her little face was beet red.

"Because, Leena, Doonie and Bianca are my fuckin' children. How the fuck can you possibly expect for me to play a part in the murda of they fuckin' mama and still be able to look at them? You got any idea the kinda pain that shit would cause my son, to lose his mama? And you want me to be the reason? Is you fuckin' stupid, lady? I love that lil nigga more than I love myself. How the hell you go be screamin' you love him too, but you wanna kill his mama? How you go look him in his eyes after that shit?" Leena was quiet as her mind twisted around the new aspect that he'd just brought to her attention. Killa saw her wheels turning and he started to shake his head. "Yeah, you need to think about that shit 'cause killin' Tiara ain't a option. Yo' ass need to accept that shit and let's me and you move on from here, or we can just part ways now. I love you wit' every inch of me, Leena, but I'm tellin' ya, don't make me choose between you and my kids. You'll never win, shawdy." And with that said, he walked out.

***

Killa pulled into the driveway of the townhouse in Lithonia. He was really dreading even looking at Tiara, but it had to be done. His mind wouldn't let him forget about the nigga who'd actually done the dirty work for her. Getting out of the Benz, he walked to the front door and, instead of using his key, he rang the bell. She came to the door shortly after, and without saying a word, she unlocked it and headed back to her bedroom.

Killa walked into the quiet house and closed the door behind him. Sighing quietly, he figured that he better talk to his son first. He needed to explain to him what he'd seen a couple of days ago. He headed to Doonie's room and found him sitting in his humongous bean bag chair in front of the TV playing a basketball game. He knocked on the door, and when Doonie looked up at him, happiness gleamed in his eyes for a split second before anger began to register in them. He turned back to the game without saying a single word, and Killa's heart broke.

"What's up, man, can I come in? I wanna halla at ya for a minute," he said.

Doonie paused the game and glared at his father with tears in his eyes. "How come you always tell me not to hit girls no matta what they do, but you hit mama?" he demanded quietly. "You said girls can't beat up boys so I can't hit them back if they hit me, but you hit my mama!"

Killa sighed again and shook his head as he stepped into the room. "I know, man, I know," he muttered as he sat on the bed to get comfortable. he had some explaining to do.

About thirty minutes later, when he was positive that he and Doonie were straight and on the same page, he left his son and went in search of Tiara. He didn't have to go far, he found her in the nursery sitting in the oversized rocking chair singing to Bianca, who cooed in her little baby language as her fat little hands grabbed and pulled at Tiara's hair and shirt.

Seeing what he'd done to Tiara's face made him cringe. One side of her top lip was ridiculously swollen and her right eye looked like a plum. Her neck was bruised badly from where he'd almost choked the life out of her and she just looked terrible. "Hey, how ya feelin'?" he cleared his throat and asked.

She stopped singing but kept rocking. "I been better," she rasped. "But I'm alive. Look a lot worse than it feel now," she said as Bianca started to fidget restlessly. "Here." She held her out for him to take her. "She go crazy every time she hear yo' voice after not hearin' it for a while."

Killa stepped over and grabbed his daughter. "Hey, princess," he whispered excitedly. Tiara smiled as she looked on at father and daughter, and wished that she'd had a father around while she was growing up. Killa looked at her and started to speak his mind. "Look, T, I'm sorry I hit ya and shit like that."

"Wait a minute," she shook her head and said. "Before you start apologizin' and shit, lemme say ain't no need to do it. I deserved every bit of that shit, and then some, for what I did. I'm the one that need to be sorry. But, I gotta tell ya some mo' shit, and all I ask you to do is just don't fuck me up too bad 'cause I ain't even gotta tell you this shit. I just wanna clear my conscience and put all this shit behind me."

Killa looked at his baby mama and wondered what else she could possibly have to tell him as he shook his head slowly.

"You remember that night you got shot..." Tiara began to purge her soul.

Chapter Seventeen

Jo-Jo. That was the nigga's name. That was the nigga that had robbed and shot him on Linden last summer, and the same muthafucka that he'd seen running from Leena's house after he'd beaten and tried to kill her. Killa vowed to himself that he was going to make his ass pay dearly for all of the trouble he'd caused, even if it was the last thing he was able to do. He weaved in and out of traffic, racing home to Leena to confirm that he indeed was the same muthafucka that had violated her in her home.

Parking crookedly, he hurried to their loft and let himself in. "Leena. Leena," he called out as he walked around looking for her.

"What?" she answered softly when he appeared at the doorway to their bedroom.

Fumbling in his pocket for his phone, he started talking. "Look, man, I want you to look at this picture and tell me if this the nigga that did that shit to you."

Leena frowned. "No, I don't care anymore. I'm tired of all dis shit. I'm not looking at no pictures. As a matter-of-fact, I got somet'ing to say." With a serious frown on his face, Killa gestured for her to go on. Taking a deep breath, she continued. "I been t'inking about what you said and I decided dat maybe it is best for me to just leave."

Forget a slap in the face, try a bullet to the head. Killa wouldn't have seen that one coming from ten miles away. It took a second to get himself together, but once he'd done so, he spoke in a calm, quiet tone. "What you mean, *leave*?" he asked.

"I mean," she sighed. "I need some time away from all of dis, us, everyt'ing. I just need to get away for a while."

Shaking his head, Killa frowned. "After all the shit we been through, all the shit I done sacrificed, you just go up and leave a nigga 'cause I ain't go kill my baby mama?" He started to cry.

"You ol' selfish ass bitch. I fuckin' hate you, man." He sat on the bed and dropped his head to his palms.

Hurt, Leena started to cry. "Who said I was leaving you? I ain't leaving you. I just need some time to myself for a while. I'm sorry."

"What the fuck I'm s'posed to do while you takin' this time? How much time you talkin' 'bout? A day, two days, a week, what?"

She shrugged. "I don't know, Brenton. I'll know when I need to come back," she whispered because the strength behind her voice was gone.

Shaking his head, Killa stood up. "A'ight," he said angrily while drying his eyes. "Go on and do what you go do, but remember, I waited on yo' ass day in and day out while you was in that fuckin' coma. I don't know how much mo' waitin' I got left in me."

"Dat's what you call waiting?" Leena snapped, angered by what he was insinuating.

"Yo' ass heard what I said. Take it how you wanna," he snapped and turned on his heel.

"Arrggghhh," she screamed and hurled a pillow at the wall.

***

At around 6:30 that evening, Killa got a call from Leena that had him back at their loft by 7:00 p.m., and he found himself reluctantly carrying and loading her luggage into the trunk of his car. Their ride to Hartsfield-Jackson International was an extremely quiet one and seemed to take a lot longer than it normally should have.

He pulled into the drop off lane at one of the gates and got out to grab her luggage as she got out and met him at the trunk. "You ain't gotta go nowhere, shawdy," he said while pulling her

Louis Vuitton suitcase from the trunk. "We can do what normal folks do and just work this shit out some other kinda way."

Leena sighed and shook her head slowly. "I need dis, Brenton. It's better for us," she pleaded. "Just let me go, and hopefully, when I come back, we can get t'ings right." She caressed his face before he kissed her deeply.

"I love you, Mileena," he whispered after breaking the connection.

She smiled sadly. "I know," she said quietly and let her gaze linger on his face for a few moments before turning and walking away.

Killa watched her retreating backside and snapped a picture with his mind. Her black Gucci jeans, Red Bottom pumps, leather summer jacket by Gucci, and then she was gone, disappeared through a door some guy was eager to hold open for her as she rolled her suitcase along beside her. He sighed deeply and climbed back into his car.

***

"Listen, Leena, I got ya. You know that's big bruh, I ain't 'bout to let shit happen to him. Just be cool. Bruh go be a'ight." Bam paused to listen for a second as Leena explained something to him. He nodded his head and moved the curtain aside in the living room of the trap spot to look outside. "A'ight. Look, he just pulled up so I gotta go, but I got ya, man. Just hurry up and come back. You know my nigga love ya, shawdy. Y'all can work this lil shit out," he said and disconnected the call before getting up to go outside. "What's up, homie?" he said as he walked up to Killa and dapped him.

"Shit. What's hap'nin? What shit lookin' like?"

Nodding, Bam dug in his pocket for a cigarette. "Everything Gucci." He paused to fire up his Newport. "I got a line for that nigga Rico. One of my pahtnas know a ho he been stayin' wit since he got out. He inboxed the numba to me on Facebook." He blew out a stream of smoke and looked at Killa's face, trying to read his expression. It revealed nothing.

"You called him?"

"Hell naw," He said with a frown. "Only talk I got for that bitch ass nigga is some gunsmoke but I know you ain't tryin' to do that so I was just waitin' to let you know about it."

Killa nodded. "C'mo," he said and headed towards his car. Once he and Bam got in and closed the doors behind them, he took out his phone and asked for the number. It took Bam a few moments to get the number out of his phone, but once he did, he called them out and Killa dialed.

He hit a button and the sound of a ringing telephone reverberated through the interior of the car.

"Hello?" a woman's voice answered.

"Can I speak to Rico?" Killa said as he looked at Bam questioningly, wondering if they had the right number.

"Hold on."

A few seconds passed and then a man's voice came over the line. "Hello?"

Killa cleared his throat and shot a nervous glance at Bam before he spoke. "This Rico?" he asked.

"Yeah, who this?"

"Aye, look, man, you don't know me, but my name Killa."

***

At one point, trying to make peace with Rico had seemed like a good idea, the logical thing to do in light of the very recent revelation of Tiara's actions. Never did Killa even consider that once privy to all of the facts of the matter, it would have a negative effect on Rico, but boy was he wrong.

Upon hearing that his only brother and sister had been murdered, along with many others, and not to mention the fact that his ace was sitting in Rice Street waiting to go down the road with a life without parole sentence, all for nothing. Hell no, that shit didn't sit right at all with Rico. He didn't giva-fuck who had done what, as far as he was concerned, they still had to answer for Nico and Trencia, and Monk and everybody from his side that had been killed or affected in any kind of way by their stupidity. And in a not too kind way, he let Killa know just that before he hung up on his stupid ass.

It was infuriating to know that all of the shit that had already happened had been for nothing, because of a fucking mistake. Rage burned through him at a fever pitch. His heart was pounding and his breaths were fast and deep as he stared off into space. It was waaay to fucking late to be saying, "We sorry for what happened. Let's be friends and forget about it."

He started to shake his head as he picked the phone back up. He wanted to know exactly who this nigga Jo-Jo was.

***

With tears in her eyes, Leena stared stared out of her window as her plane climbed, leaving Atlanta behind, along with Killa. Once she could no longer see the lights of the city, she pulled her shade down and leaned her head back against the seat. It was peaceful and quiet on the plane, and she closed her eyes to take advantage of the opportunity to do some thinking.

Killa had called her selfish, and that, more than anything else he'd said to her, had bothered her the most. Why? Because absolutely, without a shadow of a doubt, when it came to the particular situation they were dealing with, it was the truth, the whole truth, and nothing but the truth. But weren't her feelings justified? Wouldn't anybody in their right state of mind feel exactly the same as she did if they'd been subjected to the same things that she had? Shit, Killa himself had even said that he felt like the bitch needed to die. So what the fuck was the problem?

With a shake of her head, she sighed and burrowed down into her first class seat to get a bit more comfortable. She had a long flight ahead of her.

Chapter Eighteen

By the time Jo-Jo ended the call, he honestly didn't know how he should feel. He'd heard a million and one stories about the nigga, Rico, and although he wouldn't be considered a slouch when it came to the gunplay, he knew good and well that his track record just didn't weigh up against Rico's.

That was why, for the life of him, he couldn't understand why Rico, a fucking living legend in the streets of Atlanta, had called and talked to him, and seemed to regard him as somewhat of an equal.

He smirked and gave a little arrogant shrug. "Jo-Jo, boiii, ya startin' to move up and make a real name for yaself, boiii," he drawled, his smirk slowly turning into a grin as he picked up his pistol. "Just me and you, Nina." He kissed the barrel of his Sig and said, "Just me and you girl."

***

A few hours later, he was pulling into one of the parking lots of Turner Field. And by a stroke of good fortune, he found a spot just big enough to park. He cut the engine and left the A/C running as he pulled out his phone.

Hearing the unmistakable, thunderous Indian chant of close to fifty thousand Braves fans, he smiled and mumbled to himself, "Get 'em Braves." Then he hit the speaker icon on his phone. He vaguely recalled seeing somewhere that the night game they were now playing was the last of a four game series against the Yankees, but that was neither here nor there because Rico had just answered his phone.

"Hello?

"Aye, I'm at Turner Field now, bruh," he said.

"Where at?"

"I'm parked in the gold lot, up here by the statue of Hank Aaron."

"A'ight, say no mo'. I'm on the way down there now. Gimme a few minutes," Rico said and hung up.

***

Earlier that same day...

"Tiara, girl, what the hell happened to yo' damn face?" Ms. Tina exclaimed as she held the screen door open for her daughter, who was carrying baby Bianca in her car seat, and Doonie, who trailed them.

Tiara shrugged dismissively. "It ain't really nothin', mama, Killa..."

"Killa did this to yo' face?" she asked, shocked at first, and then enraged.

Tiara nodded. "Yeah, but I deserved it. I made him do it..."

"Bitch, if you don't shut the fuck up wit' all that stupid ass shit, you sound like a damn fool. It ain't shit in the world you could'a did to make that boy do this shit to you."

Begging to differ, Tiara sighed and dropped her head. "Mama..."

"Mama my ass! You called the police? I'm 'bout to call the police on his stupid ass," Ms. Tina continued her tirade as she turned in search of her phone.

"Mama, please, this shit been happened, and it's over wit'. He apologized already and I forgave him. Please, just chill, everything a'ight now."

"No fuck it ain't. I don't care how much he do for you and my babies, that stupid muthafucka ain't 'bout to be hittin' on you, girl." She closed her eyes and shook her head to keep her tears from falling. "Uhn-uhn, uhn-uhnnn, not my baby, not my lil girl, fuck that," she said and then bit her bottom lip.

Tiara understood exactly where her mother was coming from, but she didn't know the entire story, so she took a stand against her. "Ma, please," she shouted to get her full attention before lowering her voice. "Just leave it alone. If you call the police, I'ma leave and you ain't go have no proof of what you sayin'. I'm askin' you to, please, just stay outta this and trust me when I say that everything straight," she finished with a pleading look on her face.

Ms. Tina stared defiantly at her only child for a few seconds before sighing and pulling her into a hug. "If he hittin' on ya, Teet, you don't need him," she said quietly, trying to hold back her tears. "I done been through that shit before. You a beautiful girl, Tiara, you can find another nigga, one that won't put his hands on ya, baby."

Tiara smiled sadly while shaking her head. "I'll never want nobody else, mama," she said quietly. "I don't care what he do, I'ma always love Brenton."

"I know, that's why it's so sad," Ms. Tina said and turned to walk away as she thought about how much her young daughter had yet to learn.

***

Present time...

Jo-Jo didn't like his current situation at all, and he liked his current company even less. Whatever dreams he'd been entertaining about elevating his street cred had shamelessly been shattered quickly after Rico got into the passenger seat of his Buick. The impression that he'd gotten from talking to the nigga on the phone had turned out to be completely wrong, and it seemed as if he was actually lucky that Rico hadn't spazzed out completely on him.

Now, against his will and wishes, he and Rico sat in his Buick parked on John Street a few car lengths behind Tiara's Mercedes. He wasn't a bitch, but to let the truth be the told, Rico's larger than life legend was having an effect on him. He didn't want any kind of problems with him, and that was why his meager attempts at protesting had proven futile. He lit his fourth cigarette in ten minutes and glanced nervously over at Rico.

"Heads up, nigga," Rico said and tapped him on the knee while nodding for Jo-Jo to look. "Who that is comin' out the 'partment?"

"That's Tiara and her mama. That's her lil boy and her lil girl prob'ly in the car seat she carryin'," he said as he watched Rico pull a pistol off of his waist. "What you doin', man, I thought you was at her baby daddy?" he asked with panic and fear in his voice.

Rico looked at Jo-Jo with murder in his eyes and said, "This bitch 'bout to get it, too." And with that, he got out of the car.

Jo-Jo didn't know what to do. He wanted to stop Rico some kind of way, but he knew he couldn't. He wanted to yell out for Tiara to run or something, or crank his car up and just leave, but he knew that either of those actions would probably result in his demise much sooner than he'd be willing to agree to, so he looked on in outright fear as the scene unfolded before his eyes.

***

Tiara saw him approaching but she thought nothing of it until she saw the pistol clutched in his hand. Her heart started to beat a little faster, but she didn't panic. She didn't know the nigga, so even though he was walking with a gun in his hand, the chances of him doing something to her or her family were slim, so she continued on towards her car, albeit at a brisker pace than before. She had just reached to open the back door when the sound of quick footfalls made her look up.

"Mama, watch out," Doonie yelled.

"Tiara," Ms. Tina called out. But it was too late.

Boc. Boc. Boc. Boc. Boc. The nigga stood maybe ten or so feet away from Tiara as he let his shots off. When the first bullet struck her in the throat, she reflexively dropped the car seat and her hands shot up to her wounded neck. Ms. Tina ducked back into her apartment and Doonie scampered away from the barrage of bullets towards Gray Street. By the time the nigga emptied his clip and ran back to the car he'd come in, John Street was eerily quiet, a little quieter than it should have been after that particular shooting.

Ambitious

Chapter Nineteen

Killa chuckled at something Sherrelle said as he tossed a few dreads out of his face and answered his ringing phone. "Yeah?" he drawled.

"Brenton you gotta come over here now. Tiara and the baby, I don't know where Doonie..."

He pulled the phone away from his ear and looked at the screen. "Ms. Tina, calm down, slow down. What's wrong? What about Tiara and the baby?" he said when he put the phone back to his ear.

"Don't fuckin' tell me to calm down, nigga. Somebody done shot Tiara, Brenton. Her and the fuckin' baby. They fuckin' dead."

"What? What the fuck you just say?" he exploded and jumped up from the couch he'd been stretched out on at the trap spot on Linden.

"Just come now," Ms. Tina screamed and hung up.

He stared at the phone in his hand for a few seconds, dumbfounded expression and all, his more than stable mind refusing to even begin to grasp the news that he'd just heard. It took for Sherrelle, with an extremely worried expression on her face, to ask him what was up to bring him back to reality.

"Bam," he shouted and jumped into motion. "Aye, Bam!" He patted his pockets in search of his keys as he looked around the room frantically.

"What's up, big dog?" Bam said as he walked into the living room, drying his hands on his shirt.

"C'mo, ride wit' me, bruh," he said as he walked out of the door.

Bam looked at Sherrelle for an explanation. "I don't know what the fuck goin' on. He just got a call and snapped," she said.

Eager to find out what was going on, Bam nodded and headed out of the door behind his pahtna.

***

"The only reason I'ma do this shit is 'cause whoever that nigga was, shot that baby. That shit fucked up. I couldn't stand that bitch Tiara. She thought she was better than everybody, but he ain't have to kill that lil girl, too."

Detective Murks rolled her eyes in a very subtle way for her partner, Detective Stillwater, to see. "Sure, ma'am, we greatly appreciate your cooperation," Stillwater was saying to the extremely unattractive but vital eyewitness to the double murder. "Hopefully, our sketch artists down at the station will be able to put together a drawing, with your help, that we can begin to circulate to help us catch this guy. If you don't mind, ma'am, would you please go with this officer? He'll take you down to the precinct," he said while ushering the only witness, so far, that was willing to cooperate with their investigation, towards a uniformed police officer and his idling squad car.

Once their witness had gotten into the police cruiser, Detective Murks shook her head slowly as she and her partner looked on while the CSI Technicians worked. "It's turning out to be another bloody summer," she said as they saw a black Mercedes, identical to the one the victim drove, glide to a stop a few feet from where they stood.

In Detective Murks' opinion, both of the young men that got out of the car were handsome, although they looked distraught. And when they were allowed into the victim's mother's apartment with no hesitation, she and Detective Stillwater glanced at each other and headed in that direction.

The scene inside the small apartment was a combination of sadness and activity. All of the uniformed officers wore somber expressions as they walked to and fro through the apartment, and the victim's mother still hadn't been able to get her sobbing under control. A little boy was crying relentlessly with his face buried into the stomach of one of the two young men that had just shown up. Detective Stillwater waved over one of the uniforms. "Who is that?" he asked quietly with a nod towards the guy patting the little boy's back, trying to console him.

"Apparently, he's the long-time boyfriend, slash fiancé, and father of the victims two children," he nodded and said with a grimace and shake of his head.

Detective Murks visibly cringed and whispered, "He just lost his fiancée and infant daughter." While shaking her head slowly she asked the uniform, "Who's he?"

"A friend of the fiancé," he replied.

"C'mon, let's go on over," Stillwater said reluctantly with a sigh. Eighteen years as a homicide detective and still the worst part of the job for him was talking to the family of the victims.

As the two detectives made their way over to the grieving relatives of the deceased, the young man with dreadlocks looked up and made eye contact with Detective Murks. She realized right then that in all of her thirty-eight years of living, she'd never seen a pair of sadder looking eyes. After another sigh, Stillwater began to introduce himself and his partner.

***

As the detectives talked more and more with Killa and Doonie, the conversation became more and more interesting to all parties involved. Come to find out, Doonie had gotten a good look at the gunman before he started shooting, and the detectives thought that it might be a good idea to have him sit with a sketch artist also, and then compare the drawing with the neighbor's description.

That sounded pretty good to Killa because, although he'd struggled to not do so, he couldn't stop entertaining the idea that

Leena might've had something to do with it. If so, never in a million years would he ever forgive her, that is, if for some odd reason he didn't kill her ass. But he was really thinking of a couple of other people that might be suspect, mainly the nigga Rico, or maybe even the nigga Jo-Jo that Tiara said was blackmailing her. If Doonie or this other chick put a sketch together that matched either one of them, or anybody else that he knew, he vowed to himself that it was going to be real fucking bad for whoever it might be. He agreed to allow Doonie to sit with a sketch artist. Then he, Bam, Ms. Tina, and Doonie followed an officer to a nearby precinct.

It took maybe thirty minutes or so before they were finished with the drawing and, to the officers' surprise, the sketch of the guy Doonie described looked very similar to the sketch of the guy the other witness had described. The detectives showed both sketches to Ms. Tina, who agreed that the guy could've possibly looked something like the drawings, but she just wasn't sure. When Bam and Killa were shown the sketches, Killa's breath immediately but unconsciously caught. Being the veteran detectives that they were, Stillwater and Murks noticed the sudden subtle intake of breath and shot each other quick furtive glances before Stillwater took action.

"Uhhh, Mr. James," he said as he put his hand on Killa's shoulder and began to usher him towards an open room. "You mind if I speak to you for a second in here?"

Murks had already began to occupy the remaining three with random questions to give her partner time to question the fiancé about any possible information he may have about the murders or the identity of their possible suspect.

***

"How'd it go?" Murks asked as she approached her partner, the relatives of the two victims had just been allowed to leave the station house.

Stillwater sighed deeply and shook his head slowly, a grim expression contorting his face. "Not too good," he responded while leaning back in his chair. Murks took a seat in the other chair that was in the interview room. "I know for a fact that this guy knows what's going on, but what I can't understand, for the life of me, is why, after losing his fiancée and infant daughter like that, why wouldn't he want to help us catch whoever did it?"

In response to her partner's statement/question, Murks said thoughtfully, "The fiancé didn't strike me as a bad guy."

"What, you think he was in on it somehow?" Stillwater interrupted with a small frown, his gut rejecting that possibility immediately.

Taken aback, Murks' head snapped backwards a little and a frown creased her face. "What? Hell no. The complete opposite actually," she said as her face relaxed and the wheels of her detective mind began to turn. "I was saying that he didn't give me the bad guy impression, street and hood definitely, but not the type to do his fiancée and daughter."

Stillwater stared at his partner for a second, waiting for her to continue. "How is any of that relevant to him knowing what's going on but not coming clean?" he asked after she made him assume that she was through speaking due to her silence.

A small smile touched the corners of her mouth. "You losin' ya edge, old man?" she said affectionately to her partner of five years.

Stillwater smirked good-naturedly. "How so?" he asked, sitting all four legs of his chair on the ground and leaning forward.

Ready to oblige him, Murks got up and began to pace wall to wall of the small interview room. "On a scale of one to ten, how convinced are you that the fiancé recognized the person in that composite drawing?" she asked.

"Ha," Stillwater laughed. "About a hundred."

"Yeah, me too. Now tell me, and be completely honest with me, Still. If someone were to kill Miriam and Bethany and you honestly believed that you could get to the person that did it, do him, and get away with it all before the police could catch him for it, would you?" She stopped pacing and looked at her partner for his answer.

He was shaking his head slowly as he thought about someone murdering his wife of close to twenty years and his seventeen-year-old daughter. His answer was obvious, but just for the sake of clarification, he said, "In a heartbeat."

Murks began to pace again. "I know, right, I'd do the same about Kevin and Tyus. But this is exactly what I think we're dealing with here. Some guy murders the fiancée and infant daughter, right." Stillwater nodded in agreement. "And as I said, the living fiancé gave off an overwhelming street life, hood persona, but was clearly, unquestionably grief stricken and devastated." Stillwater nodded in agreement again. "So by him knowing this guy," she tapped one of the composite drawings on the table in front of her partner two times, "and being the Street Nigga that he is," she said, making air quotations when she said street nigga. "What other choice does he have other than to, as they say nowadays, 'keep this shit in the streets'?" Stillwater was still nodding slowly in agreement as he pictured and agreed with the picture his partner had painted for him. "The only question now is what do we do about it?" she asked with a sneaky little expression on her face as she cut her eyes over at her partner.

Stillwater began to shake his head from side to side as a frown spread over his face. "I hate this shit," he mumbled, but loud enough for his partner to hear.

"What's that?" she asked.

"This mutherfucker," he nodded towards the composite sketches on the table, "kills a young mother and her infant child in cold blood and, while her fiancé is willing to exact a little vigilante justice, here we are, got to try to save this mutherfu..." With a big sigh, he bit his bottom lip hard instead finishing his statement as utter fury enveloped his face.

"We could always just let it happen." Murks suggested, letting on to how she'd really been feeling ever since she'd put everything together.

Stillwater seriously contemplated the idea for a second and then sighed. "Nah, too risky."

"Then what?" she suggestively challenged.

Completely against what he wanted to do, he did what he knew his job required of him to do. Grabbing the sketches as he stood up, he said, "I'ma go see if I can get a positive ID and then a warrant on this loser. Then I'ma talk to Captain and see if she can make it top priority, spread the sketches through the entire department and surrounding counties. As much as I hate to, we gotta find out who this asshole is and get him off of the streets, for his own good and for justice."

"You're a better man than me, Still," Murks said to her partner as she began to follow him from the interview room. "I'd let his ass get shot down in the middle of the street like a rabid dog if it was up to me."

***

As soon as Leena deplaned in Spokane, she took her phone off of airplane mode and headed to the rental car desk. Although she'd tried to sleep on the four hour flight across the country, she hadn't been able to. Her thoughts hadn't allowed her that luxury. Now, all she wanted to do was get to her hotel and get some rest. She knew she had a long day ahead of her tomorrow with getting into the federal prison to visit her father.

Her phone alerted her and she ignored it as she approached the rental desk. but the sheer number of alerts that followed prompted her to excuse herself for a brief second from the rental agency clerk, who was ever so subtly attempting to flirt with her, to check her phone. Nothing on the planet could've prepared her for the nuclear bomb of a text that she read from Killa, and by the time she finished reading and re-reading it, she had tears in her eyes as she started to rush over to the flight desk.

"Hey, what about your car?" the rental clerk called out as she watched Leena speed off.

"Fuck that car, dyke bitch," is what she meant to say in English, but instead, it came out in a burst of Patios, unknowingly. The only thing on her mind was knowing that her baby needed her and getting back to him. Everything else would have to wait, including visiting her father.

She booked a red-eye back to Atlanta, which was scheduled to take off in twenty minutes, and headed towards the boarding gate.

***

"Killa, you tellin' me my baby girl did and caused all of that?"

He stared into Ms. Tina's once beautiful but now haggard looking face. "I swear, ma. You been knowin' me since me and Teet first got together and you ain't never, not even one time, known me to hit that girl. But when she admitted everything that I just told you, I just lost it, ma. That's why she was swol' up like that. That's why this fuck nigga kilt her and my fuckin' baby," he said as anger crept into his voice towards the end of his statement.

Tears began to leak from Ms. Tina's eyes again as she cried quietly. This, by far, was the saddest day of her fourty-one years of living, without a doubt. Sniffling as she tried to regain her composure, she asked, "So what now?"

"Mufuckas 'bout to die, ma," he said quietly while shaking his head and attempting to dry his eyes with his hands.

Ambitious

Chapter Twenty

Leena's Delta flight landed at a little after five, and after checking for Killa's whereabouts, she rented a car and sped to their loft. "Baby?" she called when she let herself in just before six.

"Yeah," she heard him grunt from somewhere deeper in the loft, and she went in search of him.

She found him in their bedroom stretched out across the bed on his back.

The electric curtains were drawn and the room was dark, except for the TV, which he'd somehow managed to freeze a still photo of Tiara holding baby Bianca at what looked to be a Bar-B-Q on a bright sunny day. Although she had hated Tiara, she could understand why Killa had chosen the picture. Tiara looked extremely pretty and little Bianca had on the cutest little bib that said, "I'm Here Now, Bring on the B-B-Q." She even had little Bar-B-Q sauce stains on the bib and around her mouth.

"Oh baby," she said as genuine tears sprang to her eyes. She went to Killa and laid down beside him. "I'm so sorry, baby," she said as he buried his face in her bosom and, for the first time, really cried. She cradled and consoled her man for hours, it seemed, long after his heart wrenching sobs ceased and it became clear that sleep had overcome him. Then and only then did she deem it okay for her to shut her weary eyes to sleep.

***

The sound of a ringing phone woke her from a deep, dreamless sleep. She opened her eyes just as Killa walked into the bedroom naked and the phone stopped ringing.

"You finally done woke up. Yu was ti'ed as hell, wasn' ya?" he said quietly as he pulled on a fresh pair of Polo boxer-briefs.

She nodded. "Yeah, I hadn't been to sleep in a while. How you feeling, baby?"

"Not too good, right, but I'ma make it," he said as he put the top back on his deodorant and turned around to face her. "Where you went yestaday?"

Stifling a yawn and giving a big stretch, she said, "Washington. I was gonna visit my dad today. I was at dee airport in Spokane when I got all of your messages. Caught dee first t'ing smoking back dis way. What dee fuck is going on, babe?"

Killa visibly cringed as he thought about the events of the past twenty-four hours. After he explained what had happened, all Leena could do was shake her head.

"What are you going to do?" she asked.

"You already know what's 'bout to happen, Leena," he said quietly with a raised eyebrow.

She nodded her head slowly. "Yeah, I guess I do. If I t'ought dere was somet'ing I could say to try to stop you..."

"It ain't, so don't," he interrupted her, but she kept talking.

"I would. But I know it's not, so I won't. Just be careful, baby," she finished quietly.

"I am," he said while starting to put the rest of his clothes on. "Get ya pistol, bae, keep it wit' ya at all times. I don't care if you usin' the bathroom, shawdy, have it wit' ya. I don't know how long I'ma be gone, but I'ma try to handle this shit as quick as possible. I don't want you to leave this 'partment unless you got to, Leena, and if you do, you need to have that pistol in yo' hand, cocked, and off safety. You understand me? You ain't safe because of who you or yo' daddy is, you in just as much danger as I am until I can murda this fuck nigga, so I need you to act like it. Here." He grabbed a pen and something to write on and scribbled something quickly. "If somethin' happen to me, you need to halla at whoever you need to halla at for this nigga to get wacked." It was Leena's turn to cringe, and she did so, visibly, at the thought of something happening to him as she accepted the paper he handed her with a scared look on her face. "Serious business, Leena, I done kilt this nigga brutha, susta, and some of his pahtnas, and as you can see, he don't too much care 'bout who he get at, tryin' to get back at me. Ain't no safety 'til this nigga dead, shawdy."

She glanced at the name he'd scribbled on the paper before looking back at Killa and asking the million dollar question, as far as she was concerned. "Why can't I just have my dad do it now?"

He frowned slightly and shook his head. "I need to be the one," he said quietly. "This bitch need to die by my hands, bae. That's the only way this shit go be right, but if somethin' happen to me, then his ass still need to die so you can be safe." Leena nodded but had a confused frown on her face. She really didn't understand what was so important about who killed the nigga as long as his ass got killed.

"A'ight, I'm 'bout to dip. Come lock me out."

She got up and trailed him to the door, but stopped him just as he reached to open it. "Killa," she said. He turned and saw that she had tears in her eyes and that she was trembling. "I love you so much, Brenton, I'm scared to lose you." She wrapped her arms around him and laid her head against his chest.

"I love you, too, Mileena." He hugged her and smoothed her hair down before kissing the top of her head. "I'ma be a'ight, bae. You just be careful. Keep that pistol wit' ya and don't open the door for nobody."

She sniffled and nodded *okay*, and just like that, she watched, possibly for the last time ever, him walk out of the door.

Ambitious

Chapter Twenty-One

All conversation ceased when Killa pulled up and parked in front of the trap spot on Linden Avenue that afternoon. There was a gang of hustlers posted on and around the low brick wall, and all of them wore somber expressions.

"What up, big dog, you a'ight?" Loose asked, sympathy dripping from his tone and expression.

A sad look on his face, Killa nodded. "Where Bam at?" he asked somberly.

With a slight grimace at the pain he knew his pahtna must be going through, Loose nodded towards the apartment. "Him and Reek and them in there."

When he walked into the apartment, he saw guns and boxes of bullets everywhere. Chop's were on the couch, and all types of pistols cluttered the coffee table and the counter tops in the kitchen. Sherrelle, with a pair of booty shorts on, unconsciously had her ass tooted up in the air as she bent over reaching to get something from the bottom of the refrigerator. Bam and Reek came walking from the back of the apartment then, and when they saw Killa, Bam immediately cut what he'd been saying short and addressed Killa.

"What's up, big bruh, you good?" he asked.

Killa grimaced and shook his head slowly, looking away as tears filled his eyes.

"Damn, Killa, baby, I'm sorry," Sherrelle said with tears brimming in her own eyes as she came over and hugged him.

Bam even blotted a few of his tears away with his shirt before he began to nod. "I got some news, though, bruh," he said and sniffled a little before continuing. "I got the drop on both of them fuck niggas, Jo-Jo and this bitch Rico. This nigga Jo-Jo stay in a 'partment out there in Chappell Forest."

"Chappell Forest, where that's at?" Killa asked pensively as he stepped away from Sherrelle's embrace and cleared space on the couch to sit down. He knew that he knew where it was located, but his mind was drawing a blank at the moment.

"Right there off Bankhead," Reek said. "Come outta Overlook, go straight 'cross Bankhead, and that'll put ya on Chappell Road. Go on up a lil bit and the 'partments sit right there."

"On the left. Okay, I know where ya at now," Killa said.

"Yeah, I had went over there and peeped around a lil bit, right," Bam said. "Put a lil plan together, we can fuck that boi world up tonight, bruh, if you wit' it."

Killa thought about it for a second. Rico was the main one on his mind, but Jo-Jo's ass had to get it, too, so why not now? "What ya got, shawdy?"

"I had put Sherrelle on the nigga, right." Killa looked over at her and she raised both of her eyebrows while nodding her head slowly.

"Me and the nigga been inboxin' each other all day on Facebook. He been all on my Instagram and shit. He think me and Meek go let him fuck us."

"Way I see it, big dog, we can pull up over there and lay on the nigga. Have Relle give the nigga the go ahead to slide through, and when he come out the 'partment, we can give that busta the blues."

Killa began to nod his head as he thought about it. It sounded like a pretty good plan. Without saying anything, he got up and went to the refrigerator, got himself a Peach Slice soda, and turned to face Sherrelle with a slight frown on his face. "You know twelve be checkin' that social media shit, right?" he said while pointing at her.

With an unconcerned expression and shrug of her shoulders, she said, "So. After y'all lay this nigga in the dirt, I'ma wait 'bout a hour or so and then hit him up on Facebook cussin' his ass out for not comin' through. Twelve ain't go think nothin' of it, even if they do look at it. I got this shit. Don't worry 'bout me if y'all go do it," she said confidently.

Killa nodded again and was just about to say, "Let's do it," when gunfire erupted. But it was only one shot. Regardless of that fact, everyone that had common sense in the apartment had dropped to the floor, and when they started to get up, they saw Reek, terrified expression on his face, holding one of the sticks with steam slowly rising from its barrel. One of the hustlers that had been outside came rushing through the door of the apartment with a strap in his hand and a worried expression on his face while Sherrelle just looked at her baby daddy and dropped her head.

"Bruh, what the fuck you doin'?" Killa snapped with a frown on his face. "What the fuck you got goin' on, man? You know what," he said as he shook his head along with one of his hands. "Don't even worry 'bout it. Get the fuck out," he said, pointing towards the door.

"It was a accident, man, I ain't mean to do it," Reek started helplessly before Bam cut him off, although he used a much nicer tone than the one Killa had used with him.

"Bruh, why is you even touchin' them shits? Them ain't no toys, bruh. And yo' ass just sat right here wit' me and watched me wipe all these fuckin' guns and bullets and shit for prints. We 'bout to kill some shit wit' these straps, fool." He shook his head. "Just gone outside, homie."

"But I ain't mean to do it, bruh," he said. He'd put the choppa down and raised both of his hands, palms up, along with both of his shoulders helplessly.

"Yeah, you already done told us that shit, bruh, but still, man, just go on out there wit' Loose and them, man, get out the house," Killa said as he walked over to the couch. "Le's do it, bruh," he said to Bam, picking up a box of bullets and the stick that Reek had just fired.

***

"What you think about killin' that nigga mama, big bruh?" Bam asked Killa as they sat in the parking lot of Chappell Forest Apartments, backed into a parking spot a couple of spaces over from the champagne colored Buick Lacrosse that he knew belonged to Jo-Jo.

"I don't know, man, I ain't even tryin' to think about nothin' right now besides Swiss cheesin' this nigga, bruh. After this, I can think about that nigga Rico," he said as his latex and cotton gloved hands used a grey bandanna to wipe the choppa that was in his lap for the umpteenth time. Unsure about this part of Bam's plan, he asked, "You sure about leavin' the straps out here when we done wit' this nigga?"

Bam scratched his leg while answering. "Yeah, bruh, it's better to just leave them than risk gettin' caught ridin' wit' them or gettin' caught wit' them later on. That's why we got on these gloves." He held his own double gloved hands up for Killa to see. "And you done 'bout wiped a hole in yours so I know ain't no prints on that mufucka."

"Hmph." Killa smiled a little, a bit embarrassed as he tucked the bandanna in his pocket.

"I wish this nigga would hurry the fuck up," Bam said, glancing at the clock. It was just after two in the morning and it had been about thirty minutes or so since they had used a prepaid cell phone to call Loose and have him relay the go ahead to a standing by Sherrelle, once they saw that the nigga Jo-Jo was in his apartment.

Close to ten more minutes passed by before Killa tapped Bam on the arm. "Look alive, boi, we got action," he said with blood lust in his eyes and voice as thoughts about what this bitch ass nigga had done to Leena and his unborn child, along with how he had blackmailed Tiara, and the video he'd posted of her sucking his dick raced through his mind.

"That's right, nigga, come on out to meet the fuckin' reapa," bam mumbled anxiously to himself as they watched Jo-Jo lock up his apartment and begin to walk towards his car.

They both cocked their weapons, and when he Jo-Jo reached to open his car door, they sprang into action. Killa approached from the back of his car while Bam came from the front. "Aye, Jo-Jo," Killa called.

"Yoooo?" he responded in a relaxed and comfortable tone. He was no doubt at ease thinking that he was about to have a three-way with two bad bitches, but boy was his ass in for a surprise. He looked to see who had called him, and when recognition dawned on his face, he tried to duck.

"Lights out, bitch," Killa growled as he opened up the A.K.

Bam got in position and quickly followed suit. Automatic gunfire lit up the parking lot of the Chappell Forest apartment complex, and the night. And this time, knowing that he had the right man, revenge was bittersweet. Bam emptied his fifty rounds into the nigga who looked as if he was pinned to the inside of his car door, dropped the choppa right where he stood, and ran to get the car started as planned. By the time Killa emptied his one hundred round magazine and dropped his stick, the passenger door of their not yet reported stolen Mercury Marquis was open and directly in front of him when he turned around. He quickly climbed in and he and Bam sped off into the night.

***

"What ya got, Sarge?" Detective Murks said as she and her partner, Stillwater, ducked under the crime scene tape in Chappell Forest.

Sergeant Willows of the APD's Zone One graveyard beat grimaced and shook his head. "It ain't pretty," he said and nodded for the two detectives to follow him. "Somebody really had a hard on for this kid, hundred and fifty shell casings found."

"What?" Murks exclaimed in a whisper while frowning as Stillwater gave a low whistle and shook his head slowly.

"Yeah," Willows continued. "Hundred and fifty. And from the looks of our guy, he was an unlucky enough bastard to get every single one of 'em." He stopped walking but nodded for the detectives to go on. "Y'all go 'head, I seen enough," he said with a wary expression, standing his ground just out of sight of the massacre as the two detectives rounded the back of the car to get a look at the carnage.

It didn't take long for them to be satisfied, only a few seconds, and Stillwater immediately looked around for a place to dump his coffee and Styrofoam cup. He doubted that he could stomach anymore of it, not after what he'd just seen. "This guy been ID'd?" he asked.

"Yeah..." Willows started but was interrupted by Murks.

"How?" she blurted out.

"Had his license and a couple grand in cash on him in the wierdest of places."

"Where?"

"In his shoes under the pads. Anyway, names Joseph Brown. Black male, age twenty-five, sole resident of that apartment right there." He pointed unnecessarily to the only apartment that was bustling with police activity at three in the morning. "This car is registered and insured in his name, oh-nine Buick Lacrosse. No witnesses. Nobody saw a thing."

"With the way he's minced, did you expect otherwise?" Murks asked.

"Given the location, I didn't expect otherwise, ma'am," Willows retorted. "In my opinion, this looks like a professionally done hit," he said while scratching the bridge of his nose with his thumb.

"What makes you say that?" Stillwater asked, his curiosity piqued.

"Well, I'm no detective, but this kind of reminds me of a scene from the movie *The Godfather*."

"Oh yeah? Which scene?" he asked as Murks discreetly rolled her eyes.

"You know where Pacino knocks off the chief of police and the other gangster guy. They made a big deal about him leaving the gun there. Well, that's what happened here. The murder weapons, two AK-47's, left sitting right here on the crime scene."

"They been dusted for prints?" Murks asked interestedly.

"Yes, ma'am. Both of 'em dusted, both of 'em as clean as a whistle. They were wiped before use."

"What about the shells?" Stillwater asked.

"Too many so Crime Scene bagged 'em, sending 'em to the lab for dusting, but I'm not holding my breath. I'm betting that they're just as clean as the two assault rifles. Whoever did this meant business. I'm just wondering what this kid could've done that was so bad to deserve what he got," Sergeant Willows said rhetorically with a slow shake of his head.

"You and me both," Murks said absentmindedly as the details of another random crime hovered near the edges of her mind.

***

At around 10:30 that morning, Murks and Stillwater both were in the office that they shared, catching up on paperwork, when a knock sounded at the door. After Stillwater gave whoever it was the okay to enter, in stepped a bald headed, handsome, giant of a man.

Lieutenant West, formerly Sergeant West until very recently, greeted them. "Mornin' y'all."

"What's up, Lieu," Stillwater said.

"Hey, Lieu, look at you, got ya bars on and all shiny," Murks teased him about his recent promotion.

West blushed slightly. "C'mo, Murks, cut it out."

Stillwater chuckled. "What can we do for ya, Lieu?"

He reached into the left cargo pocket of his pants and pulled out a piece of paper. After unfolding and popping it so the creases in it would relax, he held it up with his left hand for both of the detectives to see. "I know him," he said, pointing at the paper with his right index and middle fingers.

"Really?" Stillwater asked.

"Seriously. You know I'm the best we got with remembering names and faces. This guy's name is Ricardo McAllister, goes by Rico. I arrested his ass last year at a little cesspool over on Fulton Industrial. Bring him up," he said, prompting the detectives to search their database for a Ricardo McAllister.

"Damn sketch is good. I'ma try to get 'em a raise," Murks said as she compared a copy of the sketch that was on her desk to the face that was emblazoned on her computer screen.

"I second that motion for a raise for sketch," Stillwater said, his eyes darting back and forth between his own computer screen and a copy of the composite drawing.

"Told ya," West said. "But look, and this is the thing, since he's not exactly a fugitive, me and my boys can't go get him. But if you guys really want him, I suggest that y'all halla at Captain and get her to network with Nixon over in Zone Three. Have her put some pressure on him to have our guys over there bring this guy in."

"Why Zone Three?" Stillwater asked, looking up from his screen.

"McAllister ain't from the West Side, he's from the three. Summer Hill, I believe, but don't quote me on that. It may be Mechanicsville or Lakewood, but I know it's over in that area."

"'Preciate it, Lieu, big help, man," Stillwater said, nodding enthusiastically.

"No problem. Y'all let me know the second this guy goes fugitive. I'll pick him up for ya," West said as he turned his giant of a frame to leave.

"We'll let you know," Murks said, with the double murder over in Herndon Homes back on her mind again.

***

"Hey, baby, how you feeling?" Leena answered her phone, relieved beyond measures when Killa called her through the video chat app, IMO.

"I'm makin' it. What you doin'?"

"Sitting up here watching a movie, trying to keep my mind off of worrying 'bout you."

"Where that pistol at?" he asked.

"I got it right here." She picked it up out of her lap and held it in front of the camera for him to see.

"Good, I was just checkin'. Come let me in."

"You been out dere all dis time?" He nodded as he watched her walk through the loft to let him in. She swung the door open and said, "Why you didn't just knock or use your key?"

"'Cause I wanted to make sure you keepin' that gun wit' ya. This shit for real." He bent and kissed her lips before making his way into the loft. Checking the time, he headed straight to the living room and turned the TV on to channel two.

ABC's twelve o'clock news segment was just coming on as he called for her to come to him. The violent murder that occurred overnight at the Chappell Forest apartment complex was still the top story as it had been on every news segment that had aired up to that point. By the time the story had been completely reported, a few tears had leaked from both of their eyes as they still stood in front of the huge flat screen, hugging each other.

"I love you, Brenton. T'ank you," she mumbled into his chest.

"I love you, too, bae," he said and kissed the top of her head, well aware that although he could put a lot of things to rest now, shit still wasn't over. They still had a little ways to go. And if things went how he wanted, all of this shit would end real soon. As they broke their embrace, a new reporter came on the screen with a late breaking update. A mugshot of Rico popped up on one half of the screen while the composite drawing by APD's sketch artist was on the other. Apparently, he'd been deemed a person of interest in the shooting death investigation of a young mother and her infant daughter. A picture taken off of Facebook of Tiara and Bianca popped up on the screen and knocked the breath right out of Killa. New tears began to fall as he shook his head slowly and lowered himself to the couch. Leena frantically looked around for the remote to turn the TV off, and then stood in front of him, pulling his head to her and cradling it as he cried with his face buried into her stomach.

"It's go be okay, Brenton. I'm here for you. Let it out." *I'm your rock now, baby,* she thought compassionately to herself while holding her head back and looking up at the ceiling, fighting with every inch of herself to keep her own tears from falling.

***

"Got-damnit! Stupid son-uva-bitch!"

"What up, Akhi? What's wrong?" Abdun-Nasir asked his Muslim brother Abdul-Kabir.

"Akh, you ain't go believe this shit, man," Monk said to his young Muslim brother from Simpson Road as he fought hard to try to control his temper.

"What's up, akh, and quit cussin', bruh, it's displeasin' to Allah."

Shaking his head, Monk said, "I know, man. I was just so mad when I seen that shi... I mean, when I seen that junk, akh," he said, able to restrain himself from cursing that time.

"What you saw?" Nasir asked, opening a bag of The Whole Shabang potato chips and offering Monk some.

"How 'bout this nigga wanted for killin' that girl and her baby over there in Herndon Homes the other day," he said and crunched into a potato chip, still shaking his head.

"Who?"

"My lil young pahtna I took this time for."

"Nawwwwww!"

"Yeah, akh," he said with a disappointed frown.

"Didn't you just get a money receipt from this nigga?"

Yeah, he just put a band on my books the other day."

"Dang, akh." Nasir shook his head.

"I know, right. I hope they put that nigga right in here if they catch his ass. I'ma whup that nigga ass for bein' stupid, akh. And ass ain't no cuss word either."

Nasir smiled. "I might just help ya jump on that nigga. He need it. That nigga stupid."

"Yeah, he is."

A few moments passed before Nasir got Monk's attention. "C'mo, akh, it's time for prayer," he said, standing up while closing his chips.

"I'm comin', gimme a minute," he said as he thought about his current position. It wasn't good, but at least he was back on the Deen after so many years of being astray and disobedient. "Alhamdulillah," he muttered to himself while getting up to go offer Wudu.

Ambitious

Chapter Twenty-Two

"Damn, it's a lot of fuckin' police ridin' 'round this mufucka," Bam said aloud to himself as he watched the sixth, since he'd started counting, Zone 3 police car slowly cruise by him while he dialed Killa's number. He was in Sherrelle's tinted out Honda CR-V on Bass Street in Summer Hill, parked a few houses up from some broad named Zarianna's house. According to one of his pahtnas, this was where the nigga Rico was holed up. "What's goin' on, big bro?" he said as soon as the phone was answered, not giving Killa the chance to say hello. He heard his pahtna sniffle through his stuffy nose and breathe through his mouth.

"Shit, man. What's goin' on?" he replied.

Bam shook his head, Killa sounded like he had a bad cold, but he knew that it was because he was or had very recently been crying. "I'm over here in Summa Hill, right, got a bead on this nigga Rico. The way twelve ridin', though," he shook his head slowly as if Killa could see him, "Ain't no gettin' to this nigga wit'out gettin' caught."

Killa cleared his throat before he spoke again. "That's 'cause the nigga wanted for killin' Tiara and the baby. It ain't been five minutes since I just seen that shit on the news. Huh? Nah, I'm straight, bae," he said to Leena, who'd quietly asked him if he wanted to eat something.

"Say no mo'. I'm 'bout to head to the spot, right, see if I can map some shit out on how we can get at this nigga ass wit'out gettin' caught."

"That's a bet. I'm 'bout to head that way, too. I got ta have this nigga, bruh."

"I already know, fool," Bam said before disconnecting and cranking up the little SUV.

***

The taser idea had been Killa's while the idea for the chloroform, as ingenious as it was, belonged to Bam. They had put in a speedy request for the anesthetic with Killa's junkie friend, Dr. Roy Swanson. And less than two hours later, he had personally delivered two nine ounce, glass bottles of the liquid to the trap spot on Linden Avenue, complete with instructions on how to cause loss of consciousness or even death with the substance. All of that had transpired what seemed like eons ago. Now, Killa and Bam both were lying in wait, crouched behind a row of three herby curby garbage cans at the top of Zarianna's driveway.

Loose sat in the driver's seat of a ninety's modeled Lincoln Town Car in the exact same spot that Bam had been in earlier that day, awaiting the go ahead to execute his portion of the plan. "Y'all boi's get low, man, I think," he said and paused for a second before continuing. "Yeah, that's them, y'all. I don't know if he still in the car wit' her, but y'all niggas be ready," he whispered with anxious anticipation before hanging up the call. Now thinking about how, after watching Rico and the broad Zarianna get into her Camaro, and letting Bam and Killa out, it would have been a better idea for him to tail them just to make sure that she didn't drop Rico off anywhere. "But now, it's too late for all of that type of good thinking," he said to himself and took a deep breath before blowing it out through his clenched teeth.

When the Camaro turned into the driveway, its headlights illuminated the three garbage cans from the front, casting humongous shadows on the brick face of the house. Killa and Bam both were crouched as low as they possibly could, but that still didn't stop them from trying to make themselves even smaller, all the while being careful to not let any part of themselves be visible through the little cracks between the garbage cans.

The headlights of the car went out and then its engine died. They heard two doors open and then slam shut, followed by what was unmistakably the conversation between a man and woman. Killa's nostrils flared unconsciously and as the woman was saying something about how good the 4-4 pays, he jumped up from behind the garbage cans with his action being mimicked immediately by Bam. Scanning quickly, he located the duo on the landing of the front porch, the little porch light illuminating them both clearly enough for him to see the chick digging around in her purse, which was still hanging from her shoulder, as Rico sat on the railing directly behind her, holding the screen door open for her with his outstretched leg and foot.

He swung his taser that way, the infrared sighting of it grabbing hold of Rico's right thigh, and squeezed the trigger. "Fuck nigga," he growled.

The sudden movement made Rico snap his head to his right, but by the time he realized what might've been happening, it was too late. He felt something bite into his leg and heard a clicking sound that he knew, although he couldn't quite place it, an instant before he felt the hot voltage surge through his body.

"Ahhh," the woman with him screamed, though not much louder than a whisper. Her panic and fear enveloped brain had all but snatched away her ability to speak.

Bam trained the infrared sighting of his taser on her and squeezed the trigger. It sank into her cleavage and the electric current blew through her body just as she pulled a little two-shot Derringer from her Hermes purse. The little pistol fell from her hand as she crumpled to the ground and spasmed right beside Rico. "Stupid bitch, I'ma kill ya," he muttered to himself as he kicked the pistol away from her reach.

Thinking of Leena then for some reason, Killa said, "Nah, bruh, she did what anybody else would'a did. Just put the bitch out."

Nodding, Bam pulled a plastic 20 oz. soda bottle from his pocket along with a rag. He soaked it with half of the chloroform and then smothered her nose and mouth with it, knocking her out almost instantly. "What about this nigga?" he asked, standing back up and fixing his shirt, which had ridden up while he was bent over handling his business with the chick.

Killa looked down at a moaning Rico, clicked a little lever on the taser to release the electric cables, and pulled the trigger. Blue electricity sparked, accompanied by a clicking sound, before he bent and touched it to Rico's cheek. The nigga spasmed uncontrollably and made little gurgling sounds that he took immense pleasure from for a few seconds before he stopped and stood up straight again. "Now put his ass out."

He called Loose, and a few seconds later, the Lincoln whipped into the driveway and parked behind the candy red Camaro with black racing stripes. He hustled up to his two pahtnas while carrying a new roll of silver duct tape and zip ties. The three of them made quick work of taping and restraining Rico, then depositing him in the spacious trunk of the Lincoln.

"Just tape her mouth, bruh, she ain't why we came," Killa said. A few minutes later, the four of them were on their way out of Summer Hill and away from the heavy police presence.

***

On the corner of Simpson and H.E. Holmes, sat a little private school for kindergarten through twelfth grade children. It was ducked off a bit of ways from the main road and could only be accessed by turning off of Simpson and following its long, winding drive. This is the place that Killa and Bam had decided was a good spot for the nigga in the trunk to meet his end after they dropped Loose off.

Not going all the way up to the school for fear of possibly being captured by security cameras, but going far enough up the driveway to not easily be seen by random motorist on Simpson, Bam bussed a U-turn in the middle of the driveway, positioning the car for a quick getaway.

According to Roy, the anesthesia, if administered properly, was only supposed to last for about thirty minutes or so, so there was no surprise to see that Rico was awake when they popped the trunk. The two of them hefted his limp body from the trunk and dropped his ass, face first, to the concrete, intentionally.

Killa put his foot on the nigga and pushed him in order to roll him over while Bam got the sticks from the backseat of the car.

Looking into the face of the bane of his existence for the past year or so, he saw unadulterated and unrestricted hatred and defiance in Rico's eyes as his own face and eyes no doubt mirrored those exact same feelings and emotions. "Bitch ass nigga, you kilt my daughta, my baby mama, and my mufuckin pahtnas, nigga," he said slowly while shaking his head as all of his pain and anguish began to transform into anger while he accepted the choppa Bam held out for him.

Rico began to get up then. Climbing to his knees, he held his head high, looked Killa directly in his eyes, and fucking shrugged.

Rage burned through Killa like a wildfire at that gesture of defiance and he had to literally restrain himself from screaming and just beating his ass to death with the stock of the choppa. It was like he'd almost been expecting the nigga to realize that it was over for him and beg for his life to be spared, not show defiance up until the final hour. No matter though, because he was on top. "This shit over wit, nigga," he sneered as he and Bam cocked their choppas and lined his ass up. "And this time, yo' ass lose mufucka."

Just as Rico was shrugging again, the first round of two banana clips ripped into and through his body. The perfect ending to all of the madness and heartaches for Killa.

Ambitious

Chapter Twenty-Three

"Second time in as many nights, we gotta stop meeting like this Sarge," Detective Murks said.

"What we got this time?" Stillwater asked and glanced at his watch. It was close to five in the morning.

"Same as last time," Sergeant Willows began as he walked his two new detective buddies towards the slaughter. "Two weapons left on the scene, both dusted, both clean. The only difference is this time, two hundred shell casings were found," Murks closed her eyes and rubbed her face with one hand upon hearing that. "And this vic ain't been identified yet. Somebody's mad as hell," he said while shaking his head. "We need to get these guys off the streets, whoever the hell they are."

Stillwater sighed and shook his head slowly. "Gonna be another long morning," he said unhappily as they approached the massacre.

***

Killa let himself into the loft quietly and found Leena asleep on the couch, curled into a little ball with the small Glock on the seat cushion beside her. When he sat down beside her, she stirred and woke. Without saying a word, she stared at him expectantly until he began to nod his head and said, "It's over wit'."

Tears of relief sprang to her eyes as she climbed into his lap and hugged him. Killing the nigga hadn't brought Tiara or Bianca or any of his pahtnas back, but it did, finally, relieve some of the pain over losing them and give him some much needed closure to the whole ordeal. He kissed Leena's cheek and hugged her tightly to him.

***

At 8:13 that morning, Murks got an email from one of her high school friends that worked in the crime lab. "I'ma run over to the lab for a second, Scotty wants to see me, says it's important," she said to Stillwater, who was doing something at his computer.

"Alright. Let me know if it's anything interesting," he said, sipping from his steaming *I Heart Police* mug.

Murks nodded and yawned before heading for the door. Before she could reach it, a rookie detective named Fung, he was Asian, knocked on the open door and poked his head in.

"Guess what?" he said.

"What?" Stillwater and Murks both replied in unison.

"You know the guy that bit it over at the private school last night?"

"What about him?" Murks asked.

"His prints just came back, he's been ID'd."

"Spit it out, newbie," Stillwater growled.

"It's the guy from the other case you guys are working. The guy that killed the mom and baby that sketch drew."

Stillwater and Murks shot quick glances at each other. Great minds thought alike, even if they weren't always on the same page. "I'ma go check this out," he said to his partner as he jumped up. "Bring your ass, newbie," he growled again at Fung.

"I'll keep you in tune with what's going on at the lab."

***

"Whoa-hoah, look what the cat drug in, guys. To what do we owe this pleasure? You don't even visit your ol' lowly ex co-workers anymore," Scotty said with a smile when she saw her old boss and Mays High School friend enter the lab.

Murks giggled. "You so damn silly, girl. How's Ant and the kids?"

"They good, Teesh. Anthony want another baby."

That shocked the hell out of Murks who blurted, "What?"

"I know, right. I told his ass uhn-uhn," she said, shaking her head *No* as she and Murks hugged and kissed each other's cheeks before she sat on the empty stool beside her. "At this age, it'll take me sixty-five years to get this body back. Besides, four is enough for me. What about Kev and Tyus?"

"They're good. Ty turn ten next Saturday. We go' throw him a surprise birthday party at the skating rink over there on Cascade. Y'all should come through?"

Scotty nodded. "A'ight, info?"

"I'll email it to ya. So, what's up? What's so important?" she asked, looking around the deserted lab.

All business now, Scotty said, "You know that case where the shooters left the guns and a shit load of bullet shells? The first one." Murks nodded. "Well listen, I dusted maybe the first hundred and fifteen, hundred and twenty shells or so and came up with zipo, so I got lazy and put the rest of them aside, just knowing that they were clean, too. But when I come in this morning and find, to my dismay, a fresh two hundred shells waiting for me to dust, I decided to finish up the last of the first batch before I started on the new ones. And you know what I found on the very last one?"

"Don't say it?" Murks said while shaking her head with a smile on her face.

Scotty was nodding her head with her own smile working. "Yep. The most beautiful print I've ever lifted. No smudges, no smears, clear as a sunny May day."

"You run it?" she asked, but already willing to wage her own life that she either knew who it belonged to, or that whoever it belonged to was somehow connected to who she was suspecting.

"Nah, I knew it was your case so I emailed you. You can run it now if you want. It's a right thumbprint," Scotty said as she dug out a file from her desk drawer and handed it over. The greenish-brown shell was in a plastic baggie stapled to the outside of the Manila folder. "I'ma start back on these other shells," she finished saying.

With the file in hand, Murks nodded and headed to her old station, and while she waited for the computer to boot up, her cell rang. "Murks," she said as her eyes darted back and forth between the open file and the computer screen as she started to tap keys on the keyboard.

"It was McAllister," Stillwater said and paused for a second. "You thinking what I'm thinking?"

"More than likely," she said, waiting to see if there was a match in the database for the print Scotty had lifted.

"Good, I'm headed to see a magistrate now to see if I can get a warrant," he said and hung up without waiting for her to respond, excited to have caught a break in the case this soon.

The moment her partner hung up, an ancient mugshot of the owner of the thumbprint popped up on the screen and Murks' mind began to race.

***

Judge Maycy Brown took off her reading glasses, closed her eyes, and massaged her temples. "Detective, you're asking me to violate a man's constitutional rights based on a so called gut instinct? Is that right?"

"Yes, ma'am," Stillwater said humbly to the extremely beautiful black woman. Judge Brown sighed heavily, she knew right then that being the youngest judge in Fulton County history, although a great accomplishment, would mean absolutely nothing to her if she was grey haired and wrinkled from stress by the time she turned forty in a few years. Seeing the Judge's indecision, Stillwater spoke again. "Judge, I'm telling you, my gut is telling me..."

"Yes, Detective," she cut him off. "I'm fully aware of what your gut is telling you. But what I'm telling you, is I do not want to do this. But, a murderer is a murderer," she said with a reluctant nod of her head. "And he doesn't need to be walking the streets because of a technicality if in fact he is guilty." She sighed again and said, "Alright, but if we do this at all, we do this my way. First of all, you're asking for ninety days." She shook her head *No* emphatically. "That's entirely too long to violate a potentially innocent man's rights. I'll give him to you for thirty days. After that, you bring me an admission of guilt or some incriminating evidence, or this guy walks. Thirty days detective, and I swear, not a second longer. Second, there'll be no fugitive squads or no-knock warrants involved. You and your gut will personally apprehend this man and bring him into custody. Third, there'll be no trickery of any kind involved. You either get some evidence or a straight forward confession, or he walks. Do you understand?" Stillwater nodded. "I will not tolerate the slightest infraction of any of these stipulations, detective. You got thirty days." She then pulled a phone from her massive desk. "And just so you know, I'm marking it in the database and in my personal files." She held up her Galaxy Note and wiggled it unnecessarily for him to see. "Good day, Detective." She dismissed him without so much as another glance in his direction.

Ambitious

Chapter Twenty-Four

The day of Tiara and Bianca's funeral arrived a bit too hastily for Killa's liking, and it was an extremely sad affair. The little church that Ms. Tina had chosen to host the ceremony had filled quickly. And before long, it was packed to capacity. She had obviously either not known of, or not considered her daughter's and Killa's popularity throughout the city when she had made the arrangements. She, along with a few of Tiara's aunts, uncles, and other family members, were on the first couple of rows along with Killa, Doonie, and Leena. Bam, Sherrelle, and a bunch of other hustlers from the hood were there, of course, in support of Killa. Doonie cried constantly but quietly throughout the entire ceremony as Leena kept him hugged up against her in an effort to console him, while Ms. Tina was a rock. Killa's own tears hadn't fallen until both caskets, side by side, were simultaneously being lowered into their pits, and while tossing white roses into both graves as he, Doonie, and Ms. Tina said goodbye to their girls.

Turning to leave, he donned a pair of black-out Ray-Ban shades as he threw his arm around his son's shoulders. Leena, who'd hung back a little to give them some time to say goodbye, met the approaching trio, slipped Killa's hand in hers, and squeezed it gently, letting him know that she was there for him. The four of them made their way back to their awaiting limo without a single word being spoken until someone called Killa.

"Mr. James?"

He turned to see one of the detectives that he knew was working Tiara and Bianca's murder investigation approaching, along with two uniformed officers. "What's up Detective?" he asked, taking in his black casual attire and wondering if he'd attended the funeral.

With genuine sincerity in his tone and expression, Stillwater said, "I'm sorry for both of the losses you've endured young man. My and my partner's deepest condolences go out to you and the family of your loved ones," he said, glancing at Ms. Tina, Doonie, and Leena before bringing his gaze back to Killa. "But as much as I hate to do this, and no matter how much I believe that your reaction was justified, I'm here today to place you under arrest."

"Arrest? Hold up, homes, for what?" Killa snapped, caught completely off guard.

Stillwater nodded for the two uniforms to cuff Killa and began to speak again. "The murder of Ricardo McAllister." Leena immediately began to cry and Ms. Tina inhaled sharply as she shook her head slowly and grabbed Doonie. "Regardless of what someone does to you or any of your loved ones, Mr. James, you can't just turn into some kind of renegade vigilante and take the law into your own hands," he said with a sad grimace on his face.

"Man, I ain't kilt nobody, man. This a mistake," Killa said unconvincingly as he allowed the two officers to handcuff him, his heart beating at three times its normal rate.

Stillwater looked Killa directly in his eyes knowingly and shook his head. "Y'all, take him away," he said to the uniforms with a quick nod.

Leena was sobbing uncontrollably with both of her hands covering her face. And by then, even Doonie, who'd grasped the magnitude of what was taking place, was boo-hooing into Ms. Tina's midsection.

"Leena. Leena." Killa had to yell out to get her attention. "I ain't kilt nobody, a'ight. Get Brewster and let him know what's goin' on. You hear me?"

Leena, whose face was chili pepper red and all puffy from this latest round of crying, made the gigantic effort to swallow

218

the lump in her throat before nodding her understanding. A few seconds later, she watched Killa be placed into the backseat of a waiting police car and driven away, her heart breaking more and more the further away he got.

***

Because of some underhanded red taping done by the Atlanta Police, it took Brewster exactly seven days to get Killa to be allowed visits from anyone other than his attorney, and Leena was there at the first opportunity afforded to her. She'd been randomly selected and allowed to go up to the floor for visitation instead of having to use the video kiosk, and she made her way up to 7- North.

When Killa hit the visitation booth, the biggest, prettiest smile he'd ever seen spread across Leena's face, and at that moment, he longed to hug her more than anything else in the world. Smiling himself, he tapped the bottom of the two-way phone so that it jumped straight up off of its cradle and he caught it in mid-air, bringing it to his face as he sat on the metal stool. "Hey, babe, how ya been? Got news?" he asked.

"Hey, baby, how you holding up?" Was her response.

He grimaced a little and nodded while saying, "I'm a'ight. I'm makin' it. How 'bout you?"

She sighed. "I miss dee fuck out you, Brenton, but I'ma be alright 'til you get out."

"Get out?" He perked up a bit. "You got some news?" he asked again.

"About you getting out, no, but I know you will. I had Brewster put a million in escrow yestaday. Somebody ass is about to get bought. He's just waiting to see who it can be," she said matter-of-factly, but upon seeing his let down, she decided to hit him with the rest of the bad news just to go on and get it out of the way. "Dee Cuban's man won't touch dis case," she said, shaking her head. "He says dee Mayor's office is showing interest in it. Dey're t'inking dat it's a lot more going on dan what it appears to be. And Bam got locked up today."

"What?" he frowned. "I just talked to that nigga 'bout two, three hours ago."

She nodded her head. "Well, he just called me from intake downstairs about a hour ago and told me to let you know and to see if Brewster could help him. Dee police busted in dee apartment, he said dey got about four ounces of crack, t'irty-five t'ousand, and a gun."

Killa shook his head. "Damn, bruh."

She put her elbows on the little ledge and leaned on them. Holding her forehead with her left hand and the phone with her right, she asked, "Dee detectives still been trying to talk to you?"

"Yeah, they tried to talk to me again today."

"Brewster said don't say shit to dem. Don't even tell dem muddafuckas your name, just ask for your lawyer. He say dey ain't got shit, baby, so wheneva dey try to talk to you, you bet'ah keep your fucking mout' shut, you fucking hear me Brenton?" she warned him with tears pooling in her eyes.

A single tear rolled from Killa's left eye and splattered when it hit the little ledge in front of him. He nodded his understanding as she raised her watery, red eyes to look into his and placed her fat, stubby little hand against the glass partition that separated them. He put his hand against hers on his side of the glass and the rest of the visit seemed to pass by in the blink of an eye.

***

A couple of weeks passed excruciatingly slow for Killa and Leena, and late one night while he was sleeping, his door whizzed as it slid open. "James, you got a visit, bruh," the C/O said, stepping through the threshold of the cell.

"What?" Killa asked and blinked slowly a few times. His mind was still a bit sticky with sleep, but he knew damn well that it wasn't visiting hours.

"You got a visit, homie."

"Who is it, man?" he asked sleepily as he sat up in his top bunk.

The C/O shrugged. "I don't know, some police broad."

Killa nodded, thinking that maybe it was the chick Joy that Chop had known. She'd been stopping by about once or twice a week, when she could, to check on him and see if he needed anything. "What time it is, man?"

"'Bout three. Get ya self together, too, bruh. Brush ya teeth and shit, this police bitch bad, shawdy. Can't go down there any ol' type of way."

"'Preciate it," he nodded again and said while swinging his legs over the bunk as the C/O turned and left the cell.

"What the fuck you got goin' on, big bruh?" Killa's little eighteen year old, pipsqueak of a roommate from Campbellton Road looked up at him from the bottom bunk and asked.

"I don't know, young jittabug," he said pensively, wondering why the hell Joy was trying to holler at him at three in the damn morning. "But I'm 'bout to see." He quickly brushed his teeth and washed his face, then threw his blues on. The C/O came back, cuffed him, and escorted him to seven hundred, the little multipurpose room for the dormitories on the floor.

He saw that the C/O hadn't lied, but it wasn't Joy like he'd been thinking it was. A pair of skintight Levi's molded to thick, shapely legs and an ass that rivaled a strippers. A pair of pink and white # 10 Retro Jordans were on her feet, and she wore a white blouse that exposed a bit of, but not much, cleavage. A few curls framed both sides of her face while the rest of her hair was pulled back into a tight bun. "You can take the handcuffs off of him," she said to the C/O.

"You know we ain't s'posed to do that, right?" He looked her up and down skeptically for a second. "It's for your safety."

She pulled a yellow taser from the small bag she had and said, "It's okay. I know how to use this. You can take them off." The C/O nodded, uncuffed him, and left. "Why don't you have a seat, Mr. James." She nodded towards a chair on the opposite side of the small table that she took a seat at. Killa sat but eyed her warily the whole time. "Do you remember me?" he nodded. "From where?"

"You investigatin' my baby mama and lil girl murda."

Detective Murks nodded then, satisfied with his answer. "So, since you remember that, do you have any idea why I'm here?"

Actually stumped by the peculiarity of the visit, he took his best educated guess. "You got some news about they murda?"

She stared at him pointedly for a few seconds before saying in a smart-alecky tone, "Yeah, I guess you can say that. I came to inform you that the guy that did it is dead. But let me guess, you already knew that, didn't you?" Killa didn't say a word. "In fact, I'm almost one hundred percent positive that you made an extra effort to ensure his demise."

"I need my lawyer," he said with a forced calm.

Murks closed her eyes and shook her head quickly, causing her curls to swing back and forth a little. "No, you don't."

"Yes the fuck I do," he retorted as he sat back in the seat, folding his arms across his chest.

"No, you don't. See, I know what you did, and, I can prove it."

He scoffed and looked at her with an expression that said, *Yeah right, bitch.* Brewster had already told him several times over that they had nothing on him. That they were just going off of hunches, hoping to capture smoke with their hands.

With a glint of amusement in her eyes, Murks said, "You look as though you don't believe me, Mr. James?" When he didn't say anything, she dug in her bag, pulled out a small plastic baggie, and held it up for him to see. "You know what this is?" she asked.

Looking at the spent bullet casing, Killa nodded. "That's a bullet shell."

"Riiiiight," she stretched the word while nodding her head. "And you know what's so significant about this particular shell, Brenton?" His look of confident arrogance had begun to melt away. "It has your right thumb print as clear as day on it."

Impossible, he thought to himself. He knew the bitch was lying then. All the shells and guns they'd used had been wiped thoroughly, that, if nothing else, he was sure of. Not one single shell... his heart stopped as he thought about when Reek had accidently fired the choppa inside the apartment. He hadn't put on any gloves to replace that one, stupid ass fucking bullet. And neither did he wipe it. *I'm fuckin' fucked.*

Murks watched his features drop before he dropped his head. "Another interesting point, Mr. James," she began to nod her head again, "is that, this shell was recovered from the murder scene of Joseph Brown in Chappell Forest, exactly one night before Ricardo McAllister was murdered. Now I, and my partner, know that these murders are connected. They're too similar, the overkill, the leaving of the weapons on the scene. But I also know, and it took me a while to figure this out, that the murder of Joseph Brown is also connected to the murder of your fiancée and daughter as well. I had to backtrack a bit before it hit me. But after Ricardo McAllister murdered your fiancée and baby girl, he jumped into the passenger seat of a champagne colored car. And less than twenty-four hours later, Joseph Brown is mutilated. And get this, just as he was either getting into or out of his champagne colored Buick Lacrosse. Coincidence? I think not." She shook her head. Killa still hadn't looked up from his lap. "My partner, Detective Stillwater, wants you thrown under the jail as an example and as a message that retaliation of this sort cannot and will not be tolerated in this city. I, on the other hand, do not agree. See, what you don't know is that I, Sergeant Detective Lateesha Murks, am a wife and a mother and that I admire and respect the hell out of what you did."

Killa raised his head slowly to look at the detective and she kept speaking.

"Because I swear to god, had I been placed in your shoes, I'd have done the exact same thing."

His heart began to beat a little faster, he needed to say something, anything, to try to win her over to his side. But he couldn't admit guilt.

Murks held up the little plastic baggie with the shell casing in it, both she and Killa looking at it for a few seconds before she spoke again. "This shell is the only piece of evidence linking you to these murders, Brenton." She puckered her lips pensively while staring directly into his eyes for what seemed like an eternity. "Find something to do with it," she said, and tossed him the bullet casing.

He watched it sail up, arc, and then fall into his lap as Detective Murks put her taser back in her bag, got up, and headed to the door. Astonished, but not allowing it to show on his face, Killa watched her until she reached the door behind him and then turned back around to pick up the shell from his lap.

"I suppose that once my partner is convinced that you won't tell on yourself and that there's no evidence to hold you, you'll get out of here. Whenever that is, and whenever you do make it out of this place, you have a nice life, Brenton James. After what you've been through, lord knows you deserve it."

"You do the same, Detective Murks," Killa called thoughtfully over his shoulder without turning to look at her. When he heard the door close behind her, he looked at the bullet shell in his open palm and slowly closed his fist around it. "You do the same," he mumbled again to himself while nodding his head.

Chapter Twenty-Five
Epilogue
Three years later...

The A/C was blowing snowballs as Killa lay stretched out on the couch with his head resting in Leena's lap. She brushed his thick wavy hair affectionately as they watched Game Seven of the NBA Finals tip off. Doonie, who'd grown a whopping nine inches over the past two years came out of the bathroom holding his twenty-six month old little brother's hand. Seriously interested in basketball now and playing point guard in the AAU League with the Atlanta Celtics, he sat down and put his little brother, Brandon, who seemed to never stop talking nowadays, in his lap and started to watch the game.

Looking at the two half-brothers' interaction with each other, Leena was thinking it to be so adorable when Killa turned his head and began to speak into her six month pregnant belly like it was a microphone. "Lil girl, if you come outta there wit' a motor-mouth like yo' brutha, and don't never be quiet when you learn how to talk, yo' ass goin' up for adoption."

"Boy," Leena hissed and pinched his arm, then laughed. "Don't be telling her dat." She grabbed the sides of her stomach and spoke to the daughter in her womb. "No you ain't, baby, your dad is just playing, ain't you daddy?"

"Nope," he said and chuckled as she pinched him again.

When Stephen Curry seemed to effortlessly cross over a defender and nail a three pointer from deep behind the arch, Doonie exclaimed, "Oooooh," while pointing at the huge, wall-sized TV.

Brandon, who'd been jaw-jacking about one thing or another, cut his pointless gibberish in mid-sentence, whirled around to look up at his brother, and then whirled back around to face the TV. "Oooooh," his little voice said loudly, imitating his brother as he pointed also, and awkwardly with his thumb, index, and ring finger outstretched, at the TV.

The two adults found it hilarious, and after quick, knowing glances at each other, they began to giggle almost uncontrollably when the intercom on the little table in front of the couch buzzed. Leena leaned forward and hit the *Talk* button. "Yeah?" Killa said.

"I got this fine ass Sheriff lady and her kid down here boss," said Zo, the chief of security at The End Zone Sport's Bar and Grill.

"Let 'em up, Zo. And make sure they make it through that crowd down there safely. I don't want the kid gettin' hurt or nothin', man."

"Got it, boss," he chirped, happy to oblige the boss' request. Escorting the sexy ass red bone and her kid to the elevator would give him a little time to put his bid in with her.

When Joy stepped off of the elevator into Killa's second floor office/man cave above the sport's bar, which was located in Atlanta's Atlantic Station, she held a bag with Kelsey Junior's, (she'd named her son after his father, Chop, Kelsey Draymond Johnson Jr.) clothes in it for the weekend in one hand, and her thirty month old son's hand with her other. The instant Brandon saw his playmate, he started to fidget until he was able to wriggle free and slide down his brother's legs to go meet his buddy. "Hey, y'all, what's goin' on?" she said in greeting to everybody.

"What up, Joy," Killa responded.

All Leena said was, "Uhhn," with a roll of her eyes and neck. She wasn't too fond of Joy, but she'd never crossed the line of disrespect.

Knowing that her presence was unwanted by Leena, she dropped her little man off and, after doing and saying just enough to be polite, she quickly made tracks.

"When you go stop bein' mean to her, shawdy? That lady ain't never did shit to you," Killa said conversationally.

"Whenever dat heffa stop coming around." When Killa sighed, she felt the need to explain herself, "I know dat bitch wanna fuck you, Brenton. I seen dee way she be looking at you sometimes. And your ass bet'ah not fuck her ass eitha, nigga." She pinched and popped him at the same time.

"What the fuck is you talkin' 'bout ol' crazy ass girl? You see this shit?" he said with a helpless frown on his face and held up his ring finger, brandishing his wedding band. "This shit mean the world to m."

"Awww, dat's so sweet," she cooed before her face balled up into a hard mask and she pinched and popped him again. "Because it bet'ah, muddafucka," she growled.

With a shake of his head, Killa realized then and started to accept the fact that some things just would never change.

***

A few months after Bam got locked up, he sent word back to the hood that Trayon's bitch ass had told on him and got the spot busted. The black and whites that substantiated his accusations quickly followed. He wound up having to cop out to a ten do six for the money and dope in order for the pistol charge to be dropped and avoid having to do federal time. But if he kept his nose clean while up the way, he'd be home after doing a little over four years. Trayon went missing not long after Bam took his time and the police found his decomposing body in a thicket behind Vice City on Glenwood a few weeks later.

***

About a year and a half after Killa got out of the county, Sherrelle hit the lottery for a little over eight million dollars and she fucked with the crew the long way, giving Loose and Reek two hundred and fifty thousand each. Killa declined her offer to him but accepted on behalf of Bam and put it up for him. Sadly, about a year later, she was killed in a car accident on Ponce de Leon. Ironically, the drunk driver of a beer delivery truck with "Don't Drink And Drive" plastered as big as day on its sides, hit her Dodge Challenger head on, killing her almost instantly.

**

After fucking up a lot of the money Sherrelle had given him, Loose went on a caper that could've possibly set him straight for the rest of his life, and of all people, he chose Reek to ride shotgun with him. The move went sour, though, and the two of them wound up having to catch a hum-bug body in order to keep their own lives. Surprisingly, Reek stayed solid the entire time while they both blew trial and were sentenced to life and five, but Brewster says that they both have a damn good chance of getting their convictions overturned and seeing the streets again, due to a technicality.

**

Somehow, the police got onto Vega, but because of his contacts in the department, he got wind of it before the investigation was even able to get off the ground. His filthy rich ass completely dropped off the face of the planet, leaving the family business to be run by one of his younger sisters named Maria.

**

Through it all, the Buttermilk Bottom was still up and running, although whenever Killa slid through to check a couple of the old heads, all he saw was new faces. He doubted that there'd be a crew to come up out of Fourth Ward and leave their mark, like he and his crew had done, for a long time because, even though he could tell that a lot of the new niggas that were playing the blocks that he and his crew had helped pave the way for them to play, were hustlers, when he looked into a lot of their faces, he knew off the rip that they were missing something. They were lacking something vital, something that he and his crew had had plenty of. And when exactly what they were missing came to his mind as he turned his Benz onto North Avenue, headed home to Leena and his kids, he said it aloud to himself, "Ambition."

The End.

Stay Connected with Us!

Text **LOCKDOWN** to 22828 to stay up-to-date
with new releases, sneak peaks, contests and more...

Thank you!

Coming Soon from Lock Down Publications/Ca$h Presents

BOW DOWN TO MY GANGSTA

By **Ca$h & Jamaica**

TORN BETWEEN TWO

By **Coffee**

BLOOD OF A BOSS **IV**

By **Askari**

BRIDE OF A HUSTLA **III**

THE FETTI GIRLS **II**

By **Destiny Skai**

WHEN A GOOD GIRL GOES BAD **II**

By **Adrienne**

LOVE & CHASIN' PAPER **II**

By **Qay Crockett**

THE HEART OF A GANGSTA **II**

By **Jerry Jackson**

TO DIE IN VAIN **II**

By **ASAD**

LOYAL TO THE GAME **III**

By **TJ & Jelissa**

A DOPEBOY'S PRAYER **II**

By **Eddie "Wolf" Lee**

A HUSTLER'S DECEIT **III**

THE BOSS MAN'S DAUGHTERS **III**

BAE BELONGS TO ME **II**

By **Aryanna**

Available Now

(CLICK TO PURCHASE)

RESTRAINING ORDER **I & II**

By **CA$H & Coffee**

LOVE KNOWS NO BOUNDARIES **I II & III**

By **Coffee**

LAY IT DOWN **I & II**

LAST OF A DYING BREED

By **Jamaica**

LOYAL TO THE GAME

LOYAL TO THE GAME II

By **TJ & Jelissa**

PUSH IT TO THE LIMIT

By **Bre' Hayes**

BLOOD OF A BOSS **I II & III**

By **Askari**

THE STREETS BLEED MURDER **I, II & III**

THE HEART OF A GANGSTA

By **Jerry Jackson**

CUM FOR ME

CUM FOR ME 2

CUM FOR ME 3

An **LDP Erotica Collaboration**

BRIDE OF A HUSTLA **I & II**

By **Destiny Skai**

WHEN A GOOD GIRL GOES BAD

By **Adrienne**

A GANGSTER'S REVENGE **I II III & IV**

THE BOSS MAN'S DAUGHTERS

THE BOSS MAN'S DAUGHTERS II

A SAVAGE LOVE **I & II**

BAE BELONGS TO ME

A HUSTLER'S DECEIT I, II

By **Aryanna**

A KINGPIN'S AMBITON

By **Ambitious**

A DOPEBOY'S PRAYER

By **Eddie "Wolf" Lee**

WHAT ABOUT US **I & II**

NEVER LOVE AGAIN

THUG ADDICTION

By **Kim Kaye**

THE KING CARTEL **I, II & III**

By **Frank Gresham**

THESE NIGGAS AIN'T LOYAL **I, II & III**

By **Nikki Tee**

GANGSTA SHYT **I II &III**

By **CATO**

THE ULTIMATE BETRAYAL

By **Phoenix**

DON'T FU#K WITH MY HEART **I & II**

By **Linnea**

BOSS'N UP **I & II**

By **Royal Nicole**

I LOVE YOU TO DEATH

By Destiny J

I RIDE FOR MY HITTA

I STILL RIDE FOR MY HITTA

By **Misty Holt**

LOVE & CHASIN' PAPER
By **Qay Crockett**
TO DIE IN VAIN
By **ASAD**

BOOKS BY LDP'S CEO, CA$H

(CLICK TO PURCHASE)

TRUST IN NO MAN

TRUST IN NO MAN 2

TRUST IN NO MAN 3

BONDED BY BLOOD

SHORTY GOT A THUG

THUGS CRY

THUGS CRY 2

THUGS CRY 3

TRUST NO BITCH

TRUST NO BITCH 2

TRUST NO BITCH 3

TIL MY CASKET DROPS

RESTRAINING ORDER

RESTRAINING ORDER 2

IN LOVE WITH A CONVICT

Coming Soon

BONDED BY BLOOD 2

BOW DOWN TO MY GANGSTA